BEAUTIFUL MUSIC FOR UGLY CHILDREN

BEAUTIFUL MUSIC FOR UGLY CHILDREN

Kirstin Cronn-Mills

flux
Mendota Heights , Minnesota

First Edition
Eleventh Printing, 2017

Book design by Bob Gaul
Cover design by Lisa Novak
Cover art: Headphones © iStockphoto.com/Tilman Schreiber
         Cityscape © Llewellyn Art Department
Interior art © Llewellyn Art Department

Flux, an imprint of North Star Editions, Inc.

Library of Congress Cataloging-in-Publication Data
Cronn-Mills, Kirstin.
  Beautiful Music for Ugly Children/Kirstin Cronn-Mills.—1st ed.
      p. cm.
  Summary: "Gabe has always identified as a boy, but he was born with a girl's body. With his new public access radio show gaining in popularity, Gabe struggles with romance, friendships, and parents—all while trying to come out as transgendered. An audition for a station in Minneapolis looks like his ticket to a better life in the big city. But his entire future is threatened when several violent guys find out Gabe, the popular DJ, is also Elizabeth from school."—Provided by publisher.
  ISBN 978-0-7387-3251-0
[1. Transgender people—Fiction. 2. Disc jockeys—Fiction. 3. High schools—Fiction. 4. Schools—Fiction.] I. Title.
  PZ7.C88149Be 2012
  [Fic]—dc23
                                                    2012019028

Flux
North Star Editions, Inc.
2297 Waters Drive
Mendota Heights, MN 55120
www.fluxnow.com

Printed in the United States of America

For Amy Tipton

JOHN BURROWS IS THE NEW ELVIS BECAUSE HE PLAYED ELVIS FIRST

If radio is the medium of the ugly person, then I can live my life as a voice and the world will be perfect.

But the dead air has got to go.

Tick.

Tick.

Tick.

Tick.

While I fumble with the next CD, I attack the airwaves. "And that's Mika, with 'Grace Kelly.' Now let's have some Green Day. Here's 'American Idiot.' This is Beautiful Music for Ugly Children, on community radio 90.3, KZUK. Welcome to my show." I switch off the mic with a huge sigh.

John—my neighbor, my idol, fellow music geek, the

oldest DJ in the universe—claps my back. "Perfect! Don't worry about the dead air. You're just learnin'." John's from the South, and every so often his accent creeps in when he's excited about something. "But you gotta relaaaax … " He gestures like he's smoothing out the air. "You gotta let it floooooow." Another swoopy gesture. "Chatter and patter and let it floooow. Enjoy yourself!" He can see on my face that I'm still not buying it. "Maybe next time." He leaves the booth, probably to smoke.

If I could do radio for the rest of my life, I'd be set. But I also know it's a dying industry. Checking "radio DJ" on a high school career survey is like checking the box for "dinosaur." And commercial radio is all that programmed bullshit, so the only place it's okay to be a real DJ is community radio. I have no idea if a person can make a living at dinky little stations like this, but I intend to find out. Not here, of course—this is strictly volunteer. But graduation is soon, and so is summer. Life is soon.

John was a real DJ. He got me this show, because he keeps his DJ chops fresh at KZUK. His show is called Remember Me to Rock N Roll, and it's all the stuff he played when he was a DJ in Memphis in the fifties. He made his money in radio for forty years. I can only hope.

Then—of all things—the phone rings. I stuff my voice deep in my chest and race to grab it.

"Hello, KZUK, the Z that sucks." Maybe I shouldn't say that, but it's too obvious, given the call letters. I probably wouldn't risk it at nine a.m. on a Tuesday, but since it's 12:06 on a Saturday morning, who cares?

"No, you don't!" A perky voice answers me. "I love your show. Can you play a request for me?"

"Who is this?" I try not to let the tremor in my hands appear in my voice.

"Just a fan."

My very first show's been on the air for all of six minutes—and I have a fan? No way. "I can't do a request now, but I'll bring it next time if I have it. Uh ... what's your groove?" Dumb. Dorky, in fact.

"'In the Summertime' by Mungo Jerry. Do you know it? It's really old."

"Music nerds know every song, especially one-hit wonders." Not true, but close enough.

She laughs. "What's your name? You haven't said. I'm Mara."

John's gone, so I rush it out of my mouth. "I'm Gabe, uh, thanks, Mara, and tune in next week for your song." I hang up before things can get any stranger.

She brings my listener total to one.

Then I realize what I did: I let a stranger talk to me, and I talked back. AND I told her my name. That's a lot.

Possibly too much.

Silence again in the studio. But the KZUK promo is cued, and I just need to push the button. Not more than three seconds' worth of dead air. But I forget how short the promo is, so while I'm reaching for more CDs, the world is awash in silence.

Then I get it together. "Let's have a slow one, for you and your sweetie, from way back in the fifties. Here's 'In

The Still of the Night,' by the Five Satins." That song's for John.

It's very still outside. The studio windows are wide open, and nobody's around. I love being awake in the middle of the night. The darkness soothes me.

The phone rings again. I almost don't answer it, but I can't help myself. "Hello, KZUK, the Z that sucks."

"Gabe, I have another request."

"Mara?" My voice is high, because I react instead of think. I clear my throat to cover.

"'You Know My Name,' by the Beatles—do you have it?" She doesn't seem to notice my slip.

I clear my throat again and pull my voice lower. "Of course. Both songs next week, just for you."

"You're awesome!" She hangs up without more chit-chat, thank god. No more phone calls for me.

More songs go on, more music goes out into the night. Then I miss another cue, but this time it's not my fault. With community radio, the equipment tends to be marginal. We only have two CD players, and—of course—the one with the song in it jams on me. It takes me a second to remember what's cued up in the other one. Then a disco ball pops into my head.

"Let's finish out the show with another danceable love song, 'Da Ya Think I'm Sexy' by Rod Stewart. Boogie on, people, and I'll see you next week. You've been listening to Beautiful Music for Ugly Children on community radio 90.3, KZUK."

My voice is beginning to get hoarse from keeping it so low in my chest.

When Rod Stewart's done the Hustle off the airwaves, I plug in a tape of Marijane, the master gardener. I can't imagine people really want to garden at one a.m., but who knows? John never came back, and what he's been doing for the last fifty minutes I have no idea, but I find him outside, smoking.

"You know that's bad for your heart. And everything else. You're old." He's in his seventies somewhere, I think.

"I'm not that old, and you just respect your elders, all right?"

"Where were you all this time?"

He grinds it out with his heel, then puts the butt in the ashtray and grabs another smoke. "Driving around, enjoying the night, listening to your show." He stole my car keys. "And I was being jealous, because I wasn't that good my first night. So I was pouting."

I flip open my Zippo and light his next cig for him. "I bet you were that good. Better, in fact."

John chuckles. "You'd bet wrong. You were great."

"Maybe." I really want to believe him, because it was hard. I put myself out there, and I don't do that.

"Next time, though, you've got to say more. Tell them about you. Tell a story with the music."

"A story?" No way.

"It'll take practice, but you'll get it." He looks way more convinced than I feel.

T-Pain is in my car stereo, and we have it up loud enough

that college kids stumbling from party to party turn their heads to watch us go by. What's life without loud music in your car?

When we get home, John invites me in. We've spent many early morning moments debating the merits of Stax versus Motown—both old R&B record labels, and it's a toss-up—or Merle Haggard versus Conway Twitty—both old country legends, and it's Haggard, though Twitty has his merits and Johnny Cash trumps them all. John always wins with this line: "Look, I was alive then, and you need to get a grip. You don't know nothin' about it." Someday I'll make him debate Johnny Rotten versus Sid Vicious— both old British punk legends that he hates—and I'll win that one. Maybe.

John moved next door to us when I was ten, and, to put it bluntly, I want to *be* him. Musically, anyway. He's the only other person I know who dives headfirst into music and drowns in it. I guess you could call him my mentor. I know it seems bizarre to be hanging around with an old man, but I think of him like a grandpa. And my parents trust him, after living next to him for eight years and inviting him to a billion barbeques and Christmas parties. Plus, he's a musical god—who wouldn't want to hang out with someone like that?

John makes us peanut butter and banana sandwiches— we're huge Elvis fans, anything and everything, including PB&B sandwiches—and we sit down with a copy of *Rolling Stone* from the early eighties to argue about whether *Face Dances* by the Who (John's choice) or *Emotional Rescue* from the Stones (my choice) was the lamest sellout album for a super group.

John spends all his money on music, which is awesome for me, but it makes the rest of his life pretty empty. His living room has a couch, a chair, a table with a lamp on it, four big speakers, a killer stereo, a magazine rack for all his music mags, and that's it. But he has three bedrooms packed full of boxes and crates of music, some organized according to artist, some according to theme or place or era. At this point his rooms contain more than 2000 LPs and 45s, plus too many CDs, cassettes, eight-tracks, and reel-to-reel tapes to count. He also has a computer full of MP3s. I think my collection's doing all right—225 LPs and 45s, 320 CDs, 270 cassettes, and another giant amount of MP3s—and then I come over here and get a reality check.

He cocks his head while *Face Dances* is on. "Maybe it's okay. But these people did *Tommy*. This album blows ass compared to *Tommy*." That's the Who's rock opera.

Then I realize how long I've been at his house. "I'd better go. If my folks heard us come home, they'll be wondering why I didn't come inside an hour ago." I hand him back the crate of music I put by the door when I came in. "Can't wait for the next show." And that's true—it's the coolest thing in my life, no contest.

He waves at me before he picks up the crate. "Good night, Elizabeth." Then he disappears back into a bedroom to put the music away.

My birth name is Elizabeth, but I'm a guy. Gabe. My parents think I've gone crazy, and the rest of the world is happy to agree with them, but I know I'm right. I've been a boy my whole life. I wish I'd been born a vampire or a werewolf instead, or with a big red clown nose permanently stuck to my face, because that stuff would be easy. Having a brain that doesn't agree with your body is a much bigger pain in the ass.

I know there are ways to match things up, though I have no access to any of those ways right now, plus everything costs a ton of money, which sucks. And there are 24/7 reminders that I'm not really me, like my name. Not that Elizabeth is a bad name, but it's not what I think of as my real name. That's Gabe.

I also know people think I'm an ISSUE, and that gets really old. Any time THOSE SCARY TRANS PEOPLE come up, everybody flips out. It was even a talk show issue a while ago, the pregnant trans man and all that stuff. I get it, it's the craziest thing in the world, but it's not gross and wrong, it just is, so why do people lose their minds over it? Honestly, world, I don't care what you think. Stick your issue up your ass.

Big talk, huh? I really don't have much to bitch about. My parents love me—at least they used to, up until this last announcement—and nobody's ever beat me up. But I also stopped trying to make people believe me a long time ago. It was easier to hold it all in. But that's almost over now. I can almost breathe.

Got it, world? I'm a guy. A scared guy, though I try not

to show it, and a guy with a long freaking road ahead of him. But still. Just a guy.

I let myself out John's front door. When I step onto the porch, I notice the air: it's a little warm. But it could still snow tomorrow, you never know. Nothing like April in Minnesota, and our lovely town of Maxfield is smack in the middle of the southern part. It has zero excitement, forty thousand people, two high schools, one college, and lots of crap-ass radio stations. KZUK is the only decent one.

After I brush my teeth, I check, and John's lights are still on. Most nights he stays up even later than I do. He told me that when he was still working, his show was ten p.m. to two a.m.—not quite the graveyard shift, but not as civilized as drive time. We both like the dark the best.

Every night before I go to bed, I dust Elvis's first 45, a pristine copy from the first pressing: "That's All Right," Sun Records, 1954, with "Blue Moon of Kentucky" on the B side. No scratches, no damage, just perfect vinyl. It's on a stand, on my desk. John gave it to me, from his private collection. Some people say "That's All Right" was the first rock and roll song ever. I read online that John was the first person in the United States to play it on the radio, and when I brought it up, he denied it for three months. He's pretty modest. Even if I didn't like him as a human, which I obviously do, I would worship him for that reason only, even though I had to read it on the Internet.

Elvis gets me through. When I'm stressed, which is about 95 percent of the time, I imagine Elvis saying, "That's all right, Gabe," and it helps. If I'm really fumbling around, I think *what would Elvis do?* Sometimes Elvis answers.

I crack the windows in my room and the faint sounds of *Tommy* waft from John's house.

When you think about it, I'm like a 45. Liz is my A side, the song everybody knows, and Gabe is my B side—not played as often but just as good. When 45s were around, most DJs didn't care about B sides, but some were big hits: The Smiths' "How Soon is Now" and U2's "The Sweetest Thing," for example. We don't really have B sides anymore, since digital music wiped them out, but digital's not me. I'm analog, Wall of Sound, old school to the core, and it's time to let my B side play. My radio show is a deep new groove on it.

I want people to listen—to my show, to me—but if they don't, I don't care. I'm playing it anyway.

PAIGE BENNETT IS THE NEW ELVIS EVEN THOUGH SHE COULD GIVE A RAT'S ASS

Saturday night. I am spacing out in front of VH1 Classic, learning that "Come On Eileen" is the *Top One Hit Wonder of the 80s!* when Paige calls. She's my BFF and one of the few exceptions to my "don't talk to people" rule. It never applied to John, even when I first met him, though I'm not sure why. Maybe because he was my neighbor, or maybe because he's just that kind of friendly dude. Maybe because I saw how many crates of records and CDs he'd moved into his house. Even when I was ten I was a music fiend, but just about hip-hop.

She's bored, I can tell. "Can I come over and do homework with you?"

"Why the hell would you want to do homework on a Saturday night?" Even Paige and her 3.9 GPA don't do homework on Saturday night. Not like I was planning to do much of anything anyway. "And where's Bobby X?" He's Paige's boyfriend.

She sniffs. "Grounded."

"You can ground seniors?"

"His parents are strict."

I laugh. "So I'm the alternative?"

"I'm bringing toenail polish."

"Oh, please." I hang up.

Paige constantly tries to spruce me up, though not usually with toenail polish, because she claims I'm a fashion zero, which is true. She, on the other hand, is a fashionista, a true believer in *Vogue*, *Cosmo*, and eBay for purchasing those fashion bargains. She's rather Gwen Stefani, even down to the occasional set of bright red lips, and I have no idea why she talks to me except that we've been best friends since kindergarten. She was a fashionista even then. Her desk was next to mine, and there was always pink hanging out of it because she tied long pink ribbons on her pencils. Every other kid thought it was strange, but I admired her ability to match her pencils to her outfits. Pink is still her color, followed closely by purple.

By the second week of elementary school, I was already sure I was a freak, since I'd tried to line up with the boys one day and everyone laughed at me. Talking to Paige was a big move. The day I did it, she had six ribbons in her hair, three ribbons on each shoe, and a big fat plaid ribbon around the waist of her jeans. I'm not sure why I noticed or counted, but I remember those thirteen ribbons very clearly.

I walked up to her and tugged on a ribbon. "Nobody else has these. How come?"

"I don't know. I like them." Paige took one out of her hair and handed it to me. "Would you like one?"

"No thanks." My hair was the shortest pixie cut possible. My mom wouldn't let me use the clippers on it, like Dad did to his, but it was almost like David Hansen's, the kid who sat under the flag and picked his nose.

Paige looked entirely puzzled. "Why not?"

"My hair's too short, and the ribbon's too pink."

"Okay." Paige tied the ribbon back in her hair and that was that. Nerdy loner and popular girl, BFFs from kindergarten through graduation. Don't ask me why, because it doesn't make sense.

Kids started picking on me around third grade, when that social thing started kicking in and the packs got defined. I never fought back, but if Paige was around, she'd chase them off. And it's not like they knew the truth— they just knew I was a butchy girl who'd rather climb the jungle gym and play football than stand around and whisper. When we got to high school and everyone was focused on Friday night hookups, people would shout things like, "Hey, Liz, try some dick, you might like it!" And Paige would yell, "Stick it in your mouth!"

She looks at what I'm wearing—jeans, sweatshirt—and she sniffs. "Old Spice?"

"For that manly touch. May I be your man this evening? The man your man could smell like?" I stand back to let her in.

She's not amused. "No thank you."

We sit down at the table after we've taken two Mike's Hard Lemonades from my mom's stash, and the history papers get started. But my mind isn't here, because I wasn't kidding. I've wanted to be Paige's man since March, when I told her about Gabe. Before then, being her man was just an idea, and not one I'd let myself think about. Everybody knows you're not supposed to fall in love with your best friend. But now that Gabe is out, circumstances have changed. At least I hope they have.

I'm so insane. She would kill me if she knew. Bam. Dead on the floor.

I don't let her see, but I look at her hair. I don't know how girls manage to make it look messy and sexy at the same time, but hers is pulled into this bun thing, with spikes and escaping pieces, and she's adorable.

She sniffs again without looking up from her laptop. "The Old Spice is over the top. You smell like my uncle."

"You didn't have to come over. You can always hang out with Allison and Marta." Allison and Marta are her secondary friends, as she calls them. She says I'm her primary.

"But hanging out with you is nice, like hanging with Jack during break." Jack's her brother who's in college in Wisconsin.

"How am I like Jack?" He's a jock, on a soccer scholarship, and women wait in line to be with him.

"You play video games, throw crap on the floor, eat like a pig, hit me when you're mad. You always have. And you have the ultimate male accessory."

"Awesome stereotypes, and condoms aren't accessories. Everybody got them for Safe Sex Week. There was a huge box by the principal's office."

Paige arches one eyebrow at me. "Please. Only men have Zippos, and only weird men have Zippos with *ELVIS LIVES* on the side. Only fantastically weird men have Zippos when they don't smoke." She goes back to her laptop. "Get back to work. I didn't come over here to goof around."

"Yes you did."

"Whatever."

But my mind is done with homework. I spend more time watching her out of the corner of my eye. She chews her pen and types at the same time. Adorable.

She didn't study for her trig final last week and got the highest score in the class. She can eat a whole package of Oreos with me and not bitch about how she shouldn't have done that, she's too fat, now her clothes won't fit. And she has my back. When you get down to it, that's what matters.

"What?" Paige catches me.

"I didn't say anything." I grab a book and flip through it, because I think I'm blushing.

"No, you sighed, like really loud. What's wrong?"

Oh god. "Nothing."

She glares again and goes back to her screen. I start reading the book for real. John Quincy Adams, here I am. Save me from thinking about Paige.

About an hour later, she shuts her computer and throws her books back into her bag. "I'm done. I'm fried." A weird comment, because studying is like breathing to her. In the fall she's going to the University of Minnesota on an accelerated program for pre-med students, and they want people to start studying in the summer. And she's excited about it.

She goes and gets two more Mike's from the fridge. Hopefully my mom will forget how many were in there. "Let's talk, shall we?" She flops onto the couch and props her feet on the coffee table.

I sit down far away from her. "I did my first radio show last night." She knew I was planning it, but I didn't tell her when it was going to start.

"YOU DID? You butthead! Why didn't you tell me? Did you suck?" Paige hates to be left out, and she throws a magazine at me for emphasis.

"According to John, I was fantastic."

"What time was it? I can't believe you didn't tell me!"

"It was a . . . solitary journey. So to speak."

She's pissed. "John was with you! That's not solitary. I can't believe you didn't tell me." She likes John all right, but she thinks it's dumb we hang out so much. He needs friends of his own, she says, and he has some. But none of them are radio people. And none of them treat music like a religion—or a drug.

"You can listen next time, and I'll take you along some night. It's not like I'm going to stop any time soon. It's Friday night at midnight, by the way—or Saturday morning at midnight, whichever it is."

She sighs. "See if you're my primary anymore. Speaking of that, what're we doing for fun this summer?"

"Driving around and listening to music."

"We're not just doing that. We're shopping and going to Valleyfair and clubbing."

"You don't know I'll go to Valleyfair with you." It's an amusement park, and I can't say I like danger, even fake danger.

"And you need to get a job." Her Mike's gets gulped, then Paige burps the first line of "Jingle Bells." She's a better belcher than I am. "I'm not going to support your ass."

She works at Video Rewind, and I'm not sure why they don't change the name, except that "DVD Rewind" doesn't have the same ring to it. It's a big sore spot with my parents that I don't have a job, but working with a nametag that says *Liz* would be torture, and I'm not sure getting a job as Gabe is possible.

"I would never ask you to support my ass. Shouldn't you go home and quit bugging me?"

She takes a big gulp again. "No. And not to change the subject, but does John know you're trans?"

"Not yet." Big scary B side track.

"Are you Gabe on the air?"

"Music makes me happy, being Gabe makes me happy. They had to match up somewhere. And speaking of names, it *cannot* get out at school that I'm Gabe. Too complicated."

"Didn't John ask you who Gabe was?"

"I didn't say it when he was around." I have no guts

when it comes to John. If he rejects me, I'll lose my dealer, and I'm way too addicted for that.

"Oh please! He loves you like a granddau … grand-son." Sometimes she slips. "He'll get used to it, just like everyone else has."

"We'll see."

"You have to tell him."

"I don't have to do anything."

"Yes, you do." She sounds pissed. "You have to get on with it, even if you're scared." Then she softens a little. "If you don't tell him, you'll still be in limbo. Haven't you been in between for long enough?"

She leaves the room, and I hear the bathroom door shut. I know she's right. I promised myself I'd get on the Gabe road for good after high school. But sometimes I want a detour, to some place like Antarctica where people wear so many layers of clothes that nobody cares who you are.

I hear the flush and the water in the sink. When she comes out, she's smoothing her hair, trying to look good for her fans. If she had fans. "If you don't tell him, I won't help you with your term paper that's due next week for anatomy."

She knows I need her help. Bad. "I'll tell him."

She stops smoothing. "Do you promise?"

"Yes."

Paige's hug is immediate and fierce, and when she pulls back, she looks me square in the eye. "You are up to this challenge, and you're safe with him. You know that." She hugs me one more time. "That's why I hang out with you—you've got guts. You're a beast."

I push her away. "Oh yeah, that's me. A beast. Now scram, why don't you? I've gotta figure out a strategy and you're cluttering up my energy."

"I'm not going anywhere. Let's play with the Kinect."

We start playing this pop-the-bubble game, but my brain's already working on ways to drop the gender bomb on my hero, so I'm sucking wind and she's killing bubbles like a ninja.

"So what do I say? 'Uh, hi, John, I'm really a guy'? What about, 'Hey, John, you thought I was a girl, but silly you, I'm not'?" I pop three more bubbles while Paige pops ten. Pathetic.

"What did you say to your folks? 'Hi, Mom and Dad. I'm a trans guy, and my name is Gabe.' Or some variation of that. This is your life, dude. Your LIFE."

"If he stops being my friend, it's your fault."

"That won't happen." The smile she gives me is gentle. "You're his protégé. He won't care if you say you're a Siamese cat, as long as you hang on every one of his brilliant thoughts."

"Whatever."

When I look at her, sometimes I think I see the word *IMPOSSIBLE* printed on her forehead. Not her, exactly, though she's plenty difficult. Us. Romantically. We're impossible. But I still dream about it.

Sunday night, and Paige comes over for family dinner, which doesn't happen much, but my parents think of her like another daughter so she's always invited. Wait until they find out she's a daughter-in-law, ha ha yeah right whatever. John's over, too, which is an every-week thing. My mom likes to cook for him.

Sunday night dinner is a huge deal around here. It practically takes a signed note from the President to get out of it. Since Gabe arrived in March, jail time for treason would be better. Sometimes we go out, but tonight it's pot roast with potatoes and carrots, homemade bread, and strawberry shortcake. I wouldn't say my mom is Suzy Homemaker, but sometimes she gets close.

Tonight my seventeen-year-old brother Pete tells us about his new job at Target—he's a backroom guy in sporting goods and outdoor stuff, but sometimes kids' toys and games—and Mom and Dad nod along, like he's telling them he's discovered a new use for nuclear waste. John and Paige listen politely.

"Pass the bread, please," I ask quietly during one of Pete's pauses, but he still glares.

My mother doesn't look at me, but she hands me the bread. My dad passes the butter from the other direction. Nobody says a word.

"Do you need some jelly … Liz?" Paige's voice has a question in it, because she's not sure how to read everything. This is the first family dinner she's been to since Gabe's joined the crowd. But I'm glad she didn't blow my cover with John. She looks at me like *what the hell is going on here?* I shrug and nod at my food. *Keep eating. We can go soon.* She looks pissed, but I'm not sure if it's at me, for not sticking up for myself, or at them.

"I'm good with butter."

"Pass me that jelly, Paige, and Liz, pass me the bread when you're done, all right? I need something to sop up this good beef juice." John is my mother's biggest fan, since all he eats is ramen and the occasional box of macaroni and cheese. "Darn fine meal, Mary."

"You're too kind." She beams at him.

My dad clears his throat. "Liz, Paige, are you ready to be done with school?"

"Of course." Paige doesn't give me a chance to answer. "Nobody's paying any attention, so class is a waste of time." She smiles at me. "We were just talking about what we were going to do after graduation."

"What's that?" My mom still isn't looking at me.

"Paige thinks we're going clubbing and to Valleyfair." I roll my eyes at John, who smiles.

"Can I go to Valleyfair with you, Paige?" Pete's not one to pass up an opportunity.

"Brothers aren't allowed." Paige's smile both stops him in his tracks and makes him forget what she's said. I know for a fact he's had a crush on her since he was in fifth grade and we were in seventh.

"Maybe sometime we can all go." Dad gestures to Pete and John. "Make it a family outing."

"I'd like that, Joe." John pushes his chair back. "Thank you, Mary, for your fine food. Liz, I'll see you later." He drops his hand on my shoulder. Paige kicks me under the table.

"Girls, could you help me clear the dishes?" Mom's still not looking at me. Pete has faded into the living room, and my dad's gone into the bathroom with the newspaper. Paige and I pick up plates and glasses and follow her into the kitchen. In the fifteen minutes we help her, she looks at Paige and at the dishes. That's it.

When we're done, Paige and I go to my room.

"Your parents need to get a clue. I wouldn't put up with that shit." She huffs like they've personally insulted her.

"They haven't kicked me out yet, so that's all right."

"Wait till John comes over here and calls you Gabe while he's off on some music tangent. That'll shape them up." She digs in her bag for her laptop and her history book again. "Get out the homework, dude."

My heart shrivels up when I think about telling John. Better to do more history. I try not to watch while she chews her pen and types.

Before she goes home, I let her paint my toes. Pink. I don't know why.

SATAN IS THE NEW ELVIS SINCE NEITHER ONE EVER DIES

High school is totally A side, and I hate it. But soon, Maxfield West High, good-bye. I chant it in my head every morning: I will survive. However, I swear I will never play "I Will Survive" on my show. Well, maybe the Cake version. Then again, "I Will Survive" was a B side—and it was huge.

Graduation is soon. My new life is soon.

Eight a.m. I shut my locker so the mess doesn't escape into the hall. Aside from books and papers, there are about twenty CDs in there that would make the world's biggest crash if they landed on the floor.

Paige scurries up. "Gabe!"

"Keep your voice down." I hiss it at her.

"You look rather good today." She brushes imaginary

23

lint off my shoulder. "It's a bit more *GQ* than your traditional look. A nice change."

It's khaki cargo pants and a tailored shirt, with glasses instead of contacts. It's not easy to make yourself into a guy with just clothes and a haircut. And what sucks is I never get to have a bad day. I make it work or Gabe doesn't happen.

"Cheap, easy, and moderately stylish, brought to you by Target. What more do you want?"

"I want you to be stylish more than once a week. And wear your glasses more often. They frame your baby browns." She always tells me she likes my eyes. "You look a little bit like James Franco."

"Go to class."

She gives me a look and scampers back down the hall like a smart-ass rabbit. I see her link hands with Bobby X, and Bobby gives me a tiny nod as she chatters in his ear on their way to AP English. He's all emo-goth seriousness, with hair down over one eye and two piercings in his lower lip, and so skinny he'd disappear if he turned sideways. I have no idea what she sees in him except that he's sixth in our class GPA-wise, and Paige is third, which I've always admired in her since I'm about ninety-seventh. But he's so gloomy he makes Marilyn Manson look like a ray of sunshine.

I hate it when Paige has a boyfriend.

Bobby X did serve a purpose in my life. He's a comic book geek, a truly passionate collector, so I respect that because I know how he feels. Three weeks ago, when he was still trying to impress Paige, he made us come over so he could show her his collection. Neither of us was impressed, but we were polite. As he was digging through his boxes for his first edition of *Ultimate Spider-Man #1*—"Valued at two hundred bucks!" he told us, the only time I've ever heard anything close to an exclamation point in his voice—I saw a comic called *Beautiful Stories for Ugly Children*. My brain said, "Beautiful music for ugly children." And my show had a name.

I pass a crowd of girls on my way to geography and they look at me like I'm from Planet Strange, which is true. As I get to class, Chad Baker slams his locker door and turns to me. "Hey, he-she-it girl, s'up?"

Instead of ignoring him, my general MO, I smile. "How ya doin', asshat?" I can afford it. This life is almost over.

I'm not sure why guys are meaner to me than girls are—they don't even know about Gabe, and it's not like I'm stealing their girlfriends. Maybe on some subconscious level they know we share a label. And if *I'm* a guy, maybe they think it makes them *less* of a guy. Honestly, there's a part of me that's sad to join them. If testosterone shots turn me into an asshole, I'm gonna be pissed.

I slide into my seat in geography about a second before the bell rings. This class is sort of okay, but Heather Graves is in here, and she's Beyoncé, J.Lo, and Christina Aguilera all together. I've had a crush on her since we were freshmen. We were in the same gym class, and she and I had to be square-dance partners once since we didn't have a matched set of guys and girls. I looked at her shoes the entire time.

Mr. Anderson doesn't call the roll out loud, so I don't even know if he knows I'm here, which is fine. I prefer to be white paint on the wall—something you'd never notice. But I always stick out. Plenty of other kids take shit from everyone, but I get it double because nobody knows where to put me. Lesbian? Guy? Ugly and can't dress herself? I don't fit anywhere.

"Elizabeth Williams."

I jump. "What?"

"Come to the board, please."

"Excuse me?"

"No excuses—come to the board, please." There's a blank map of Europe, the Middle East, and Asia up there.

I stand up and bang my knee on the bottom of the desk. I hear a snicker and a "lesbo!" from the back of the room as I slouch my way up there. Two random guys I don't know are giving me the look usually reserved for dog shit on your shoe.

Mr. Anderson clears his throat. "Please label all the countries that were once part of the USSR."

"Excuse me?" I stall for more time.

"Once again, no excuses—please label all the countries that were once part of the USSR. There are fifteen countries." He sits next to the board on a high stool, straight and prim.

My hand is frozen, marker tip resting on Russia. I do know that one. I write it slowly, and my brain begins to feed me more answers. I label as many as I can, as fast as I can, and sit down. In my hurry to get back to my seat I manage to kick a desk, and a voice from the back hisses, "carpet muncher."

I bury my face in my notebook.

Mr. Anderson peruses the board. "Very good, Elizabeth. You only missed Kazakhstan. All right, class, who can tell me…" The sound drones on as I recover.

I pull my notebook away from my face and look at the picture taped there. It settles me, just a little. It's my senior picture. My other senior picture. I went to another photographer the week after my mom made me do the Elizabeth ones. Those were outdoors, and my mom wanted at least six poses with two different sets of clothes. I look like I'm going to barf in every single shot, and she was pissed beyond belief when she got the proofs. This one is more my style—soft lighting with a dark background, me in a dress shirt with a good-looking tie. I'm looking straight into the camera with no smile. Gabe the businessman. You kind of have to squint your eyes to believe it's a guy, but it's a start. It was a good day.

The photographer thought I was nuts when I asked him for only one four-by-six print. But who else would I give them to?

"Who's that?" Someone's talking in my ear. I whip my head around to see Heather. When did she start sitting behind me? Or talking to me, for that matter?

I almost can't speak. "Where'd you come from?"

"Anderson just rearranged us, remember?"

"I forgot." I'm not even sure I remember my name right now.

Heather's still staring over my shoulder. "Who's that? He's kind of cute. Hold it up."

What would Elvis do? He would show her the photo.

27

Somehow I have strength in my hand, and I lift the notebook so Heather can see it over my shoulder.

"He looks ... hey, is that you, just really butched up?"

"Well ... "

"Or is it a cousin or someone?"

"It's ... hard to explain."

"He's kind of cute."

I try not to fall out of my chair. We've never said more than three words to each other and she thinks Gabe is kind of cute. Go figure.

"Ouch!" Heather yells it in my ear. I'm sure talking to me has caused her brain to melt down into one massive headache.

"Sorry."

"Not you." I look behind me and she's picking up a pen. "Them." The two dudes with the stupid comments are waving at her.

"Elizabeth Williams and Heather Graves!" Mr. Anderson's paying more attention to me today than he has the whole semester.

"What?"

"Yes, Mr. Anderson?" Her answer is better than mine.

"Focus on the board, not on your neighbor."

"Yes, Mr. Anderson." We say it together.

At graduation I'll be the happiest senior in the history of the universe. Hands down.

Finally, finally, finally the class is over and I slouch out the door. Behind me, I hear Heather Graves yell, "Mara!"

There are bunches of Maras in this school, right? Tons of Maras.

I sneak a look to my left, and Heather and a beautiful brunette are laughing about something. I decide to casually shuffle by and see if I can hear her. She's never been in any of my classes. Maybe she's a junior.

Voice as perky as can be, the brunette says, "Do you think you'll go to Jessie's tomorrow night? I'm not sure if I want to."

I'm so lucky Mara doesn't look at me, because I'm blushing. It's definitely the phone girl, not to mention the fact that Phone Mara is also Change Girl. Every day, when I buy myself a Pepsi at lunch, I have to get change from her at the snack bar, and I always think, "Gee, that girl is pretty."

Shit.

I see Heather wave goodbye to Mara and link arms with the guy from the back of the class who threw the pen. They walk off somewhere, and Mara goes in another direction.

Note to self: buy a roll of quarters on the way home.

Seventh hour. Government. Paige is in the AP version and I'm in the everybody-else section, and we're doing group projects about the Constitution. My group has to do the Eighth Amendment, which is the one about cruel and unusual punishment. I'm not sure why group work isn't counted in that amendment. Especially when it's a group with Paul Willard and Kyle Marshall.

Well, Kyle's okay, not stupid or a bad group member, but he keeps frowning at me when I talk, like I'm speaking another language. Paul's just dead weight. He's flirting with Ashley Jones, who's actually in the group next to us, and she's got her hand on his knee. Paul's hard-on is probably keeping him from thinking about the Eighth Amendment.

Kyle kicks Paul under the table. "Hey, dipshit, you're in charge of finding three sources about the Eighth Amendment."

Paul smiles one more time at Ashley, then turns back to us. "Why can't she do it?" He looks at me.

"Liz has other stuff to do. This is your shit."

"Whatever. " He scoots his chair closer to Ashley and starts whispering in her ear.

I turn back to Kyle. "So what's my job?"

"Find three sources about why the death penalty isn't considered cruel and unusual punishment."

"Sure thing." I grab my books and go to the front of the room. Mr. Alonzo is looking through his desk for something, which I'm hoping is a breath mint because his breath is legendary.

"May I go to the library?" I stand back a bit, just in case.

Alonzo looks up at me, then at the clock. "You've got five minutes until last bell. Sit down." He goes back to rummaging through the crap in his drawers.

I go back to the table where Kyle and Paul are. They've started talking about what's going on this weekend and neither of them is paying attention to me, which is great. I watch the clock for four more minutes. When the bell goes off, Paul stands up before I can and kicks my chair. "Later, he-she-it girl. Get your sources."

"You got it, asshole."

When he turns around to look at me, I give him the finger, very calmly. He laughs, not in a nice way, and reaches out to grab my hand and break it, but I pull away. Kyle stands and watches, waiting to see the fight. Nobody moves. Paul is the first one to give, and by the time he and Kyle are at the door, he's laughing and looking for Ashley to flirt with. Mr. Alonzo doesn't say a word.

I stay back until everyone else is out of the room, and then I go home.

I will survive, jackoffs. Just watch me.

ADAM LAMBERT IS THE NEW ELVIS BUT WITH EYELINER

Friday after school, driving home, and I'm listening to the Vibe, 89.1, Your Twin Cities Station for the Cool Sound. It's commercial but way more hip, and they play everything from college rock to alt country to James Brown, with only tiny slices of Top 40 stuff. It's more like KZUK than any other station on the dial.

I'm thinking about my show later on, not really paying attention, thinking how I need to get Mara's request. Then an announcement cuts through my fog: "Want a chance to create our sound? Post your name and the titles of your top five coolest summer songs on our blog, and win a chance to compete for five thousand dollars and a seven-to-midnight weekly guest spot here at the Vibe. But here's the twist—no songs from after 1985. We want to make it hard on you. Deadline to enter is May 1. See our website for more details."

I almost wreck. Today is April 30.

Everyone wants me to go to college, of course, but I need to focus on Gabe, and a job I like ninety miles away "in the greater Minneapolis/Saint Paul metro area," as the news always says, would be perfect. Nobody would care what my name used to be, and I could start saving money for everything. My parents would kill me, but so what? They'd already like to, so one more nail in the coffin is no problem.

Someone Up There is smiling on me. Or it's way too good to be true. I don't know which.

I'm frantic when I knock on John's door. He can't ignore the pounding for very long. "Hey, Liz! Time to work on your show?"

"Not yet, but I have a question, O God of Music." My hands are shaking, and I keep hearing Paige in my ear: *You have to tell him!* Not right now.

"Lay it on me." I see the grin flickering around the corners of his mouth. He knows he's a god but he doesn't like to admit it. It's the humble thing, just like not telling me he was the first to play Elvis.

"Have you listened to the Vibe lately?"

"Sure have." A bit of a smirk.

"Did you hear about the contest they're running—for the guest spot?"

"Sure did." Now the smirk is a smile. "You're telling me this is the first you've heard of it?"

"I've been on a Jay-Z binge. Can you help me enter it?"

"No." Bigger smile.

"Why not?" Now I'm panicking.

"You're already entered." He's pulling me toward his computer. "I took the liberty of doing it for you last week, but I forgot to tell you. I'm old." He opens a browser and pulls up the website. "There you are."

There are 247 entries, and I'm number 222. The songs he's listed for me are "Summer Nights" by John Travolta and Olivia Newton-John, "School's Out" by Alice Cooper, "Wipeout" by the Surfaris, "Cruel Summer" by Bananarama, and "In the Summertime" by Mungo Jerry.

Which reminds me. "Changing the subject for just a second, I don't suppose you have a copy of 'In the Summertime,' do you?"

"Of course."

"Can I have one?"

"Of course." He motions me inside. "Not on iTunes?"

"Nope." I have no desire to explain about Mara, who I now think of as *Mara Who Goes to My School Isn't That Craptastic*, but that's not what matters now.

John goes from room to room, digging through boxes and bins. "So do you like what I picked for you?"

"The only one I would have switched out is 'Vacation' for 'Cruel Summer,' just because I like the Go-Go's better than Bananarama."

John shows me Mungo Jerry on eight-track. "Do you have time to wait while I make this into a CD?"

"Sure."

"In that case, let me put some other one-hit wonders

on there, to balance it out. 'In the Summertime' isn't very good." He goes off to make the CD and I follow along. Maybe he'll let me touch something, or read some liner notes. John doesn't allow unsupervised browsing.

While he works, I carefully examine the stuff in the crate labeled *BEST SOUL SINGERS OF ALL TIME*. There's Aretha, Al Green, Alicia Keys, and John Legend—all carefully alphabetized—plus about twenty more.

"Be gentle with those." He sees what I'm doing. When the CD is done, he pops it out. "All sorts of things for you: Mungo Jerry, 'In-A-Gadda-Da-Vida,' that stupid Soulja Boy song. Why not do a one-hit wonder show tonight? Those are always good."

"Isn't 'In-A-Gadda-Da-Vida' that metal song that sounds like a serial killer's chasing you?"

"The very same. Scary metal was big in the late sixties."

"Did you know, according to VH1 Classic, 'Come on Eileen' was the number one one-hit wonder of the eighties?"

"Give me another minute and it can be yours."

Then I realize something. "Can I see the blog again?"

"It's still up." He gestures to the computer. "Did anybody else pick Alice Cooper? The Vibe won't be able to resist that one."

"Um . . . I don't know." I'm not skimming song titles—I'm looking at names. And, of course, it's there. Elizabeth. He wouldn't know to enter me as Gabe because he doesn't know me as Gabe. Which means exactly what Paige said—it's time to tell him.

"So … are you coming with me to the station tonight?" Might as well start there.

"Not this time. I'd rather stay home and listen." He grins. "Find out how talented you really are. By the way, did you know you didn't introduce yourself on the air last week?"

"Yeah, well … " I grab the edge of the computer table to stop my hands from vibrating off my body. "My name, um, isn't Liz. So saying it is kind of tricky."

John's expression is a mixture of confusion and incredulity, with a small dose of *this person is crazy*. "Your name … isn't Liz? Have I been calling you the wrong thing for eight years?"

"No … it's just … well … I'm trans. Transsexual. Hormones, operations, all that."

His face clears. "You're a triangle?"

"What?" Maybe he needs hearing aids.

"You just said you're a triangle, didn't you?" Now there's a smile where there was a frown. "I knew someone who was a triangle."

Might as well follow along. "You did?" What the hell is he talking about?

He starts digging through a box of albums under the table where the computer sits. "Sure. Billy Tipton. Well, I'm not sure he was entirely a triangle, or if he just knew he needed to be a guy to make it in jazz." Flip, flip, flip. "Here." He hands me an album and points to the guy on the front. "Billy Tipton. Incredible piano player, used to go to his shows all the time. His real name was Dorothy, and nobody knew he was a woman until the paramedics tried to resuscitate him after his heart attack. When they took off his clothes, bam. A coochie snorcher."

"A what?"

"You know." John's blushing, just a little. "A ... bearded clam. Don't make me say the real word, huh?"

Now I'm laughing. "So he had a coochie snorcher but he lived as a guy. I can imagine that." I imagine it all the time.

John's giving me his thinking look. "Have you been a triangle all your life?"

"Transsexual. Trans man."

"Triangle, transsexual, trans man, it all starts with T. Have you been one all your life?"

"In kindergarten I remember wondering why I had to line up with the girls when I knew I was a boy."

"That says triangle to me." John's digging again in the box on the floor. Finally he stands up and hands me a K-Tel album, *Eighties One Hit Wonders*. "Here we go. Do you want more than 'Come On Eileen'? The album's digitized already. I just needed the track list to see what else I had."

"Uh ... sure." This can't be the end of it. "What I said ... it doesn't bother you?"

He fiddles with the computer a while, then puts in a CD. "You're you, and that's what matters." Click, click. "I'm sad you felt like you couldn't tell me, but I understand. It's a big thing to tell." Click and drag. "So what should I call you, getting back to saying your name on the air?"

"My name is ... Gabe." It's a relief to say it out loud. It's a bigger relief to know I can trust John. Then it hits me. "I can't do my show anymore, can I?" My heart is preparing to leap out of my body. I can't believe I didn't think of it.

"Why not?" More clicks.

"Because you told them there was a girl doing it, and now there's not." The tears are close, and I hate that. Tears are the one thing about me that's Liz.

His face is a mix again, curiosity and confusion. "I'll just tell them Liz decided not to do it, and this guy I know stepped in instead. No big deal."

"Really?" Thank god.

"And just so you know, it may take a while for the Gabe thing to sink in. I've known you as Elizabeth for a long time." Then it dawns on him. "So this is why Sunday suppers are so tense."

"You got it." Suddenly my whole body's shaking. "Uh…I need to sit down for a sec." John rolls me the office chair he's standing next to and I land on it with a whump that almost sends it sliding into a stack of music crates.

John clicks the CD out of the computer. "I know you know this, but I think of your family as my family." John always says nobody will claim him—radio and alcohol chased away his wife and kids. He finds a Sharpie and writes *one-hit wonders* on the CD. "So I'm with you all the way. Are you gonna do one-hit wonders tonight?"

"Don't know. Lately I've been stuck on the idea of A sides with successful B sides."

He rubs his hands together like a mad scientist. "Oooh, that's a good one. Let me think." He starts taking things from various crates and boxes, leaving the room and

38

coming back with more. "Let's be sure you do Rod Stewart, and probably you should do Hank Williams…" We're in our music world again, just like always.

We sort and pick for a while, flipping through boxes and crates, but I have to ask again because I really want to know. "How can you just … accept it like that?"

"I've seen a lotta things, done a lotta things, and known a lotta people." His accent is back. "The strangest person I ever met was a sword-swallower. A guy with a coochie snorcher is nothing compared to a dude who puts sharp metal in his guts. Who'd want to do that?" His face tells me that he's utterly, utterly serious. "You are you. That's all there is to it."

Nobody's ever said it like that. Not my family, not even Paige. But John is right.

I am me.

It's midnight. Between my collection and John's, I'm set.

I'm so freaked I could puke.

"Welcome, ladies and germs, to Beautiful Music for Ugly Children. I'm—uh … "

It's all right, Gabe. Now or never. It's Elvis, in my head. *You are you, remember?*

" … Well, I'm Gabe, and this week's theme is A sides and B sides. Here's a requested A side—actually a one-hit wonder—for Mara's listening pleasure: 'In The Summertime' by Mungo Jerry, right here on 90.3, community radio KZUK."

There may be three people out there, but you want each one to cheer when you put on their favorite song. "In the Summertime" is a little too midday sunshine for the midnight hour, in my opinion, but it's all about the listeners. And even bad music is good. Mostly.

The phone rings about halfway through the song.

I concentrate. My voice is stuffed. "KZUK, the Z that sucks."

"You brought me my song! What about 'You Know My Name'?"

"Coming up. It fits with the show, so I would have played it anyway."

"You're the best! Nobody ever plays my requests, not even when they're easy."

"I oblige loyal listeners."

The smile in her voice is obvious. "Can I ask for another request?"

"Sure."

"How about 'I Wanna Be Sedated' by the Ramones?"

"For that one I've got live recordings, studio recordings, and recordings by about ten other artists. Any preference?"

"Live. You are sooooo cool! Bye!"

I miss my cue again, because I'm hanging up, but "Let it Be" solemnly proceeds into the air, followed by "You Know My Name," one of the coolest, funniest B sides ever. Then two more—Hank Williams and U2—and then I think about what John said. Tell a story with the music. It's now or never.

When the song's finished, I take a deep breath.

"So tell me, listeners … are you an A side or a B side? Are you a Top Forty hit, or an equally good yet potentially undiscovered gem?" I can't believe I'm saying this. "Some of you might be right up there in the top ten, but if you're listening to this show, I'd bet you're more on the funky side." Dorky. "Then again, I think all of us have our A and B sides, even though digital music has kind of wrecked that idea."

Another deep breath.

"Personally, I like my B side, which is tough, because everybody else likes my A side. But I'm sticking to it." I feel and hear my voice shake, but hopefully it's not noticeable on the air. "And I played my B side for someone yesterday, and he was okay with it. No complaints, nothing. Can you imagine? Along the lines of loving on the B sides, here's 'Don't Worry Baby,' the B side of the hit single 'I Get Around' by the Beach Boys."

It's in the goofy CD player, so it stalls. When I almost put my finger through the *on* button, it finally obeys.

Then, when the Beach Boys are over, I risk some patter again. "I'm tired of being someone else's idea of a hit record. How about you? I know this is a radical idea, but people should get to be who they want to be. If you're going for the top of the charts, all right. A side all the way, go for it. But if I want to play my B side, I should get to play my B side. And only the cool kids listen to B sides."

I am sure Paige is whooping it up about the coolness part. If she's listening, that is.

"What about you—more A side or B side? Write it down somewhere, chalk it on the street. 'I'm Ed, and I'm a B side!' or 'I'm Martha, and I'm an A side'! Maybe you haven't decided yet. Or, on your A side you're a nice girl, and on your B side you're a hooker. I don't know. But we've gotta love all our grooves. They're the only ones we get."

I can't believe I said so much. My heart is racing and I'm panting from all the crazy nerves.

"How about a little dance music? Here's Madonna's 'Into the Groove,' which was the B side to her single 'Angel' way back when Madonna was new. Care to dance?"

I dance, too, because it feels good to shake out the nerves. But then I skip the CD, so I sit after that. Then more songs go on without chatting, because I need to chill.

Finally it's time to wind it down. "You know, life is just programmed chaos. Everybody starts out on one side—that's the programmed part. But then chaos happens, and our album flips. We get fat or thin, or dye our hair and pierce our nose. But those are just our outsides. Our insides are still beautiful, even if we think we're ugly children."

Yuck—too deep. Time to bail.

"For our last song of the night, let's get local with Prince's 'Let's Go Crazy' and 'Erotic City,' another A and B side, just for that sexy touch. I'm … Gabe … and you're listening to Beautiful Music for Ugly Children, on community radio 90.3, KZUK. Back at you next week with some more programmed chaos."

I need to remember Prince—he'd make a good show all by himself.

I jump around a little bit with the songs, especially "Let's Go Crazy." But then I skip the CD again. When the show is over and Marijane is gardening away, I get all the CDs back in the crate and get things organized. Then I step into the dark air, starting the 167-hour wait for the best sixty minutes of my week. One more groove laid down.

My phone rings while I'm driving home.

"Gabe, that was amazing! Flat out. But the A side/B side part was really strange." Paige's reaction. We chat, make plans for tomorrow, and hang up.

My phone rings again.

"Liz, that was fantastic—you chatted! You can do even more next time." John's reaction. Then there's a pause. "Gabe. I mean Gabe."

"No stress." For him, I can be patient.

"I'll get it right, I promise. Meantime, let's hear it for your B side." I can hear that he's smiling. He always says if you smile, your listeners will hear it.

"Thanks."

"Sleep well, okay?"

"You got it."

I actually feel about 15 percent peaceful, which is a huge improvement over my normal 5 percent. Then there's Elvis, very quietly, as I'm drifting away: *it's all right, Gabe. Just trust.*

We'll see.

JESUS IS THE NEW ELVIS BECAUSE HE HAS AN ENORMOUS FAN CLUB, TOO

Saturday night. Because we're bored, Paige and I decide to drive up to underage night at Happiness, a karaoke bar in Minneapolis's Warehouse District. Ninety miles isn't that far to drive for some entertainment, and karaoke is better than nothing. We get there and the place is crammed with people we don't know, which is perfect.

Paige is a brainless hoochie mama when we club— short skirt, high heels, designer handbag, and a million strands of beads. I, on the other hand, wear a button-down shirt and more dressy jeans than Levis, but that's as far as I go. No matter what I wear, no one looks at me anyway, because the woman thing turned out all right for Paige, to put it mildly. She's quite shapely, with serious boobs and nice hips. She's okay if I grab her every so often so we look like we're together, but sometimes she grabs me. And that's

45

okay too. It might be flirting behavior, but I'm not sure. Sometimes when I look at her while we're dancing, I think I see *MPOSSIBL* on her forehead. Not quite as impossible as before, but still there.

Paige and I dance a few—we're good together—but then I realize I have to pee. Bad. Peeing is normal for 98 percent of the human race, but not for me.

When I open the door to the men's at Happiness, I breathe deep and puff up my chest. Men's rooms stink way worse than women's rooms. I try to swagger, but no one looks up from the urinals. Thank god no one is in the stall—men take forever in there, so sometimes I have to go out and come in again. I pee as quickly as possible, come out, wash my hands, keep my head down, and get the hell out.

Paige laughs when she sees me. "You look like someone bit you on the ass!"

"I was in the men's."

"Brave guy! Now be my boyfriend and dance with me." Paige bats her eyes.

"I'm your boyfriend?" I don't let my voice give away the perfectness of that idea.

"Just tonight."

"What about Bobby X?"

She snaps her gum at me. "What about him?"

We head out onto the dance floor as some dude does a horrid rendition of Journey's "Open Arms," looking dreamily into the face of a guy sitting close to the little stage. I gather Paige up and we sway around the room. She flips the edge of her skirt and smiles at other couples as we go by. I know she likes Gabe better than Bobby X. Compared to him, I'm a much cheerier guy.

On our way home, I keep thinking about bathrooms because I have to pee again. Paige wants to stop at Perkins "just to see who's there, come on Gabe, it'll be fun!" I say okay, so that I can go.

Of course, when I walk into the women's, a girl jumps back and says, "Oh!" when she sees me. Then she looks again, and her face clears. "Hi, uh, Liz." It's Stacey Nelson from my government class.

"Hey." I go into the stall and do my business. I would never try a men's room anywhere in Maxfield.

By the time I get back to Paige, she's parked herself at a table of students from her AP classes and she's laughing and chatting away. I point at the door, to let her know I'm going out to the car. After being Gabe all night, I'm not interested in being Liz. As I'm walking through the door, Paul Willard and Kyle Marshall are coming in. We look at each other, we look down. Nobody's an asshole.

While Paige casts her social spell, I think about urinals. Maybe there's a way.

The next day we surf the web at her house. I love the World Wide Wonderfulness, because there are answers out there. I just have to know the right words to pull them from the ether. In this case, I settle for "trans man" and "pee" and hope for the best. I found my chest binders on the web, too—it's a trans man's shopping mall.

There are more options than I expected, and Paige is astounded. "Different shades, even!"

"You think all men's dicks are the same color?" We've never talked about dicks before. Awkward.

"Well, no, but … who knew? And they're called prosthetics, like if you lose an arm."

"What do you think they should be called? Accessories?" I click around some more.

"Don't be a dork. And I can't say this 'do is working for you." She starts fingering my hair, pushing it around, though it's not going anywhere because it's pretty short. "Why not grow it a little longer? Remember, James Franco. That's what we're going for."

I wish she wouldn't touch me like that. All the nerves in my body light up and my heart flutters, which sounds great and romantic, but it's kind of scary. "Keep your hands off my freaking head."

She stares at the screen as I scroll through the choices. "'Prosthetic' is such a … "

"Medical word? Regular word?" I keep looking.

"Well, yeah."

I consider what's on the screen, and think about what I have in my bank account. "The fact that I trust you is the only reason I'm letting you sit here."

"Except that it's my house. And of course you can trust me. And John." When I told her about John's reaction, she said, "I told you so."

"Four to six weeks to get here. That sucks."

"So? That's not long."

"In my heart, I have a penis. In my pants, I have a vagina. I want my heart and my pants to match."

She just stares at me.

"Got it?"

"What a line." Paige frowns at the monitor. "Why is it called a Mango?"

"Think about it, dork. Man-go. A man goes. He goes pee. It's a pun."

"Oh. Duh." She looks slightly embarrassed. "But won't your parents ask you why you had a Mango shipped to your house when you can go down to the store and get one?"

"Shut up!"

After everything's ordered, we go to the mall so Paige can look for an outfit for graduation. She makes me hold her purse while she tries on thing after thing at store after store. My brain starts to hurt from all her questions: "Does this color go with that one?" and "Should I get a skirt or a dress?" And, of course, "Does this make my butt look big?"

While we're walking around, I see Heather Graves with a bunch of people. She gives me a big smile and wave, so I give her the same in return. Then a random guy grabs her arm and pulls her down the walkway. It's a different guy than the one she was with after class. She forgets all about me, laughing and smiling at him.

Paige sees me wave at Heather. "You're friends with Heather?" She doesn't seem to approve. Heather and Paige run in two separate crowds.

"We have the same geography class, that's all."

"Oh." But I see Paige looking out of the sides of her eyes at me.

After I get home, I park myself in my back yard and close my eyes. It's a nice place, all landscaped and fancy. There's even a pond with a fountain that my dad built. The pond is maybe a foot deep, with built-up brick sides and various sizes of rocks sticking out of it, so the fountain will splash and make noise. It even has underwater lights.

The sound of water flinging itself over the rocks soothes me, so I pull up a lawn chair and dangle my feet in the pond while I chuck landscape gravel into it, plink plink.

"Please don't do that."

I jump about a foot. "Geez! Don't sneak up on people!"

Before my announcement, my mom was a regular mom with an amazing capacity for patience, even when I grew my hair into a six-inch Mohawk that I sculpted with Elmer's glue and/or gelatin, whichever we had. That was in my Sid Vicious phase a few years ago. After my announcement, she put every single school photo, from kindergarten to my senior picture, on the refrigerator. The night after I told them, she called her best friend and cried at least five minutes for each picture. She thought I was gone, but I was upstairs. I wanted to run down and rip up every single one, then tell her how sorry I was. I just stayed upstairs.

"Did you and Paige have fun last night?" She's standing next to me, staring into the fountain.

"It was fine. We danced. Watched people sing karaoke."

Big pause. "Did you ... go as Gabe?"

"There wasn't anybody there we know, if that helps."

She's flustered. "You know that's not what I meant." Now she's staring at the grass.

"Forget it." No use getting uptight.

"Could you please come help me with supper? John might come over too."

"Be right there."

She heads back inside, Birkenstocks making flip-flip sounds as they slap her feet. I know summer's coming when my mom wears her Birks the right way: no socks. I want to run after her and hug her like I did when I was six, when I needed her because I was scared of the thing under my bed. But I can't bring myself to do it.

Then my dad comes by and studies the pond but not me. "Did your mother tell you not to throw the gravel in the pond?"

"She did." I stand up to go inside.

"Okay." He goes back to his shop.

Then Pete comes by. "Can I use your car? I need to go to Target and check my schedule."

"Keys are on the table. Hey, Pete…"

"Cool. Thanks, Liz." And he's gone.

They've perfected the art of making me useful but invisible.

I go inside and make salad for my mom.

I hope nobody's home when the Mango gets here.

I bought a dick today. Holy shit.

This week, John and I come up with a show about sports—who knew? Before I go to the station, we throw a crate together with some pep band music, some songs about sports, and a few songs from sports movies. Nothing like the theme song from *Rocky* to get the blood pumping— gonna fly nooooooooooooooooooooooooooow.

Chatting sucks, and I sound like a complete dumbass. Nothing's flowing. I'm sure John's cringing in his living room.

I save "The Horse," a very obscure funk & soul B side from the sixties, for next to last. Maxfield West's pep band adores it for its brass parts, so I tell them I brought it for their pleasure. Then I let it slide into a version of "I Wanna Be Sedated" by the University of Nebraska Cornhusker Marching Band. We'll see if Mara hears it.

The phone rings when it's almost finished. My stomach's in knots, but I pitch my voice as low as it will go. "KZUK, the Z that sucks."

A giggle at the other end. "Who knew marching bands could play the Ramones?"

"Gotta love those obscure tracks."

"You are so cool, Gabe. Seeya!"

"Bye, Mara."

If she only knew.

On my way home I call Paige. She's out with Bobby X.

"Did you listen?" I can hear Bobby X in the background, saying, "Who's that?"

"Not tonight ... we were busy." There's a bit of a smirk in her voice, and I can imagine what they were busy with.

"Make sure you use a condom, and I'll see you later." I hear a "Wait!" before I hang up, but I'm not interested in her sex life.

I try not to be, anyway.

BARACK OBAMA IS THE NEW ELVIS BECAUSE HE'S LIVED IN A BIG WHITE HOUSE, TOO

Tuesday evening. My mom asks who I want at my graduation party, so she can send the invitations I told her not to get since they say Elizabeth. I tell her I'll pay for some Gabe announcements, cheap postcard ones or the fancy kind, whatever she wants, but her glare tells me I'm outvoted. I go to my room without giving her any names.

Paige calls. "You are never, in a million years, going to believe what I saw."

"An octopus walking down the street holding Elvis's hand."

"You fool, I saw your graffiti!"

"My what?"

She heaves a big sigh. "Remember? 'Are you an A side or a B side,' all that?"

"How do you know it's mine?" She's got to be kidding.

"Stuff like *MITCH'S B SIDE = SATAN* could have only come from your show."

"Where are you?"

"Corner of Eighteenth Street and Third Avenue."

"What are you doing out there?" It's way out in the industrial section of town.

"Taking my dad to work so I can have the car later."

"Don't go anywhere."

When I get there, I'm amazed. Seven feet high on an abandoned brick warehouse: pink, purple, blue, black, and yellow graffiti, signed by Becca, Mitch (Mitch = Satan!!), Jake, Sarah, and Maggie. The wall says this:

MITCH'S A SIDE = MITCH. MITCH'S B SIDE = SATAN!

JAKE LOVES TO JERK OFF TO HIS B SIDE

SARAH SAYS A SIDE ALL THE TIME

BECCA'S B SIDE: BOSS

MAGGIE = BOTH SIDES = EVERY DAY

The words *UGLY CHILDREN BRIGADE* are written at the top and *BE RADICAL—CLAIM YOUR GROOVE* is on the side of the mural. Everything is beautiful—swirls and pretty lines, flowers and colors everywhere. My mouth is hanging open.

Paige elbows me. "Looks like you've got fans."

"How did anybody know to listen?"

"I Facebooked it."

"Dammit!" I'm pissed. "You said you'd keep my secret!"

"You told me not to tell anybody about Gabe, not the actual show. I just said there was a cool radio show on at midnight on Fridays on KZUK and everyone should listen. If you were ever on Facebook, you could have yelled at me a week ago."

Down at the bottom of the mural there's a drawing of a trumpet and the words *PEP BAND FUCKING RAWKS! THE HORSE!*

Paige goes to get in her car. "Coming to my house, Mr. Big Shot Radio DJ?"

"Sure thing, Ms. Loudmouth." I cannot believe that wall. We go to her house and she chats at me about Bobby X and graduation and summer and college. All I want to do is run into Paige's back yard and do cartwheels, but then she'd have to take me to the hospital. *MITCH'S A SIDE = MITCH. MITCH'S B SIDE = SATAN!* Somebody listened. Holy shit.

Paige catches me. "What are you smirking about?"

"Becca and her B side." Maybe I could do a handstand.

"We didn't need to know Jake jerks off to his B side." She makes a face.

"And which Jake, not that I'm curious about who's jerking off, and Mitch who? Get your Facebook page up."

She checks. "I am friends with ... two Mitches, seven Sarahs, ten Jakes, three Maggies, and one Becca. But I don't know which of the ten Jakes are friends of Becca's. Just so you know, I'm not spending my night cross-referencing friends on other friends' pages."

I check her numbers. She has 716 friends. There are 350 people in our class, and there's another high school on the other side of town—Maxfield East—and she's probably friends with half of them, too. And probably random people in Indonesia.

"Either way, dude, you have fans." She pretends she doesn't want to smile. "Don't get a big head."

"I'm cool." But it's too late.

When I leave Paige's house, I call John. "You've got to come to the corner of Eighteenth Street and Third Avenue. Like now."

"That's a pretty dull part of town."

"Just get here, will ya?"

I go back to the abandoned warehouse and look at it some more. It's completely insane.

I take a bunch of pictures with my phone, breaking the wall into parts so I can get it all. Then John pulls up in his pimpmobile, which is a 1965 Cadillac Eldorado, just like Elvis drove.

"What's so all-fired important that you had to drag me to this ugly part of town?" He's laughing. "You got a hot date out here?"

"Take a look." I point to the wall. It's corny as hell to

57

say, but every time I look, it feels like someone put a glow stick in my chest.

John turns where I'm pointing. "Holy goddamn smokes. Look at that. Somebody's listening. Even to the sports show." After he looks for a bit, he turns back to me. "Ugly Children Brigade? That's pretty catchy."

"I know."

"So what're you gonna do now? Give 'em new directions next week?"

"Probably." I can't stop smiling.

He holds up his hand for a high five. "Gimme some skin, Liz… Gabe… sorry."

I slap him five.

"Your show this week has to be extra good." He's walking to his car, pointing at me so I'll get in mine. "Or they'll quit listening."

"So let's go practice." I slide in and put on "Rubberneckin'" by Elvis, then follow John as he pulls out.

Stop, look, and listen, world, just like Elvis says. Gabe is comin' at you, right here, right now, on KZUK, the Z that Sucks, rockin' and sockin' and blockin' your cocks off!

Maybe not quite like that.

CONAN O' BRIEN IS THE NEW ELVIS AND HE HAS THE HAIR TO PROVE IT

Friday afternoon. At 2:17 John leaves a message on my phone: "Get your butt over here after school, pronto!" I get the message at 3:12 and have to wait until 3:35 to bolt out of my seat, but I hurry my ass to John's house. Either someone's died or there's news from the Vibe.

I screech into my driveway and barely get the car door open before running across the lawn to John's.

"You don't have to break the door down, you know. The email's not going anywhere." He moves aside to let me in.

"You have no idea what this means to me."

"Oh, I might." He grins. "This is your career, Liz—Gabe—sorry. Your career, starting right here and now."

"Where's your computer?" I'm walking from music room to music room, looking for his laptop.

"On the table."

I almost don't want to read it. But I do.

Dear Elizabeth (entered by John Burrows):

Congratulations! You've made it to the final round
of the Vibe's DJ Talent Scout contest. Your five-
song summer set was quite engaging, and we're
anxious to have you compete for the grand prize:
$5,000 and a weekly guest spot (seven p.m. to
midnight) at the Vibe.

The competition will be July 12 at 7 p.m. at
Summer Mondays in the Cities, an outdoor street
festival held each Monday evening in Loring Park
in Minneapolis. Each contestant (there are five of
you) will have approximately thirty minutes to show
us your strengths. The theme for your thirty minutes
is radio songs: songs about anything that relates
to the business of radio. You may also include one
song that doesn't relate to our theme—a "secret
song," so to speak.

Please let us know if you're still interested in
competing. We'll hold your spot for five days.

Sincerely,

Thad Rosenbloom, Station Manager,
The Vibe 89.1

Holy shit.
I read it again.

Holy *fucking* shit.

"So what do you think?" John is absolutely beaming. "And a secret song to boot. I've got a million ideas already."

"I can't believe it." My whole body's tingling. It would be too perfect. I could get a place in the Cities somewhere, and a job, do the guest spot every week and meet a bunch of radio people. I'd have a parking space and an apartment that belonged to me, and I could cook food that belonged to me. I wouldn't have to talk to anyone who knew me as Liz except Paige. Maybe my family. Gabe 24/7. All of it would belong to me.

"What about… Elizabeth?" John asks. "Will the Vibe… can you … are you gonna do it as her? I didn't know, when I entered you. I'm sorry." He looks like he expects a scolding.

Oh my god. Of course.

"Yeah. No. It's okay." My body's all tingly again, but not from excitement. Shit. How will the Vibe pay me? They can't pay Gabe, because he's not legal. And Gabe can't rent an apartment or have a checking account. Shit.

"Why not just tell them you changed your name?" He points at the laptop.

"That's a pretty big name change." I could throw up.

"This is your career lookin' you in the face." His accent is creeping in again. "Professional experience, a way to make it to other stations. You owe it to yourself to ask." John is almost stern, and this is a new stance for him. We don't get crabby with each other. "Email them. Right now."

He gives the laptop to me. "I'm not letting you go home until you ask." I've never seen him this serious.

"Yes, sir." I take a few deep breaths while he stands over me, watching.

Gabe 24/7. That's what I want.

Hello, Mr. Rosenbloom:

I'm no longer Elizabeth, but I am Gabe. Can I still compete?

Nope.

I'm becoming a guy. Gabe. Can I still be a part of your talent search?

Not that, either.

John reads each line I write and then erase. "Will you please just get it over with? How many more ways can you put it?"

"You have no idea." I try one more time.

I'm transitioning from Elizabeth to Gabriel, but I'd still love to compete.

"That's exactly right." John nods. "Finish it up and call it good."

I add a couple niceties and include my email address instead of John's. My hands are shaking so badly I can barely type, but I finally hit *send*.

If the greatest opportunity I've ever had slips through my fingers because of my weirdness, I am going to lose it.

John pats me on the shoulder. "Are you ready for tonight? You'd better have something for the Ugly Children Brigade to do—you don't want them to get bored."

"All done, Chief." Tonight's show is songs about moms, since Mother's Day was last week. Dumb idea, maybe, but we'll see. They're not all country songs, either. At least I was smart enough to think about it before now, because I'm not sure I could come up with anything in the next six hours.

He gives me one more pat. "It's not so unusual to be a triangle these days. Look at Chaz Bono. He was even on *Dancing with the Stars*." John shakes his head. "Hope he doesn't do to his face what his mother's done to hers."

In spite of the shakes, I laugh. "Cher is gross."

"Go get in the DJ mindset." John's walking me to the door. "A person shouldn't be so scared of a wrinkle that they look like a plastic doll." He winks. "I like my women soft and round, not hard and brittle."

There are plenty of women who come and go from here, late at night. He thinks I don't see them, but I do. John's a bit of a catch, as my mom says, and there seems to be no shortage of older ladies trying to reel him in. According to Mom, he's got just the right amount of laugh lines, and his bald head lends him an "air of mystery." I think his best feature is his smile. It's cheerful, but kind of charming and sexy. Maybe he'll teach me to smile like that.

"Considering I've never felt a woman, I guess I'll just have to wait and see."

He looks startled for a second, then he laughs. "So you're a straight guy?"

Even though I don't want to, I blush. "Far as I can tell."

"Just don't ever choose a lady that looks like Cher, okay?"

"I promise." I head down the steps and across the lawn.

He calls after me. "You did the right thing, and it'll get easier every day. Not like I know anything about it, but it will."

There's a faint echo in my head, and I'm not sure if it's John or Elvis: *It's all right, Gabe.*

When I walk by the garage, my dad's in there staring at all his tools. The radio's blasting classic rock. It's usually that or public radio, the talk part of it. He turns his head toward me, but he's looking at the ground.

"Hey, Liz, I know I'm a little late on this, but what do you think I should make Mom for Mother's Day?" He fancies himself a woodworker, and he's not bad, but some of the stuff he makes doesn't work.

I ignore the fact that he didn't call me Gabe. "How about a clock? Maybe a simple one?" The last clock was so crazy it looked like Dr. Seuss made it.

"How about a jewelry box? It doesn't have moving parts."

"Sure. She's got a ton of jewelry."

"Then it's settled. What were you doing over at John's?"

They don't know about my show, and I'm not going to tell them about the contest. "Hanging out and talking music."

"Have you thought about a job? Not that it's bad to chat with John, but a job might be a better use of your time." Dad turns back to his tools.

"I ... um ... it's hard to imagine working as Liz when that's not me."

The storm clouds close over his face in an instant. "Getting a job is the primary issue, not what your name is."

"You have no idea what the primary issue is!" Whoops, but there it is.

"Elizabeth Mary Williams, you do NOT talk to your father like that!" My mother is there, all of a sudden, and acting like I tried to murder him with a hammer. She goes over to my dad.

Forget being nice. They're already permanently disappointed in me, so who cares? "First of all, my name is Gabe, so get used to it. Gabriel Joseph. And my name matters BECAUSE I'M A GUY. Get it right!"

Dad slams down the piece of wood he's holding and glares at it. "Listen here, young lady, having one's daughter suddenly declare she's a man is pretty mind-blowing, so just give us a goddamn chance. You may think you know who you are and what you want, but you're also young and maybe a little foolish. Besides that, it's time for you to go to college, so if you had a job, your college fund would look a hell of a lot better." He's angrier than I've ever seen him.

Instead of storming out, which is my first impulse, I close my eyes and breathe because he's right: this is hard on them. I may be young and stupid, like he said, but they're confused and hurt. Because of me.

I keep my voice calm. "Getting a job as Liz would be going backwards. I'll work on it, all right?"

I leave the garage and head straight for my room. I have seven hours until my show, so I resolve to lie on my bed and breathe until it's time to leave.

When my mom calls me for supper, I go, against my better judgment. The silence is ice cold.

Dad: "Liz, would you pass the ketchup?" Not looking at me. It's burgers and bratwurst, with baked beans and chips.

Pete: "I need a bun, Liz." Hand out, expecting me to fill it with bread. Not looking at me.

Mom: "Liz, have you made any college decisions?" Not looking at me, and apparently unaware that the deadline for all that has passed.

Me: "Nope." I was accepted at three places. They think I'm going to one of them. I'm not. College as Elizabeth would be even worse than work as Elizabeth.

Silence. Everyone contemplates their supper.

Me: "Could someone please fucking look at me?" No raised voice, just a question. Then I'm the center of attention, and their mouths are wide open.

Pete: "You're a fucking freak."

Mom: "Elizabeth and Peter! We do not use that kind of language!" No mention of the fact that Pete called me a freak, so she must agree.

Dad: "What's wrong with your head? How long have you had that haircut?"

Me: "May I be excused?" I don't wait for an answer.

I make a quick check of my email, then lie on my bed until eleven and listen to tons of metal: Megadeth, Black Sabbath, and Anthrax, with a little Motörhead for variety and that punk influence. Then I call John and ask if he wants to go to the station.

Then it's midnight, and it's my time, and I swallow. "Welcome, welcome, friends. It's Beautiful Music for Ugly Children time, right here on 90.3, KZUK. Tonight's a Mother's Day show, since it just came around—are you being nice to your mom? Getting her gifts, doing what she asks you to? Or are you making your mother crazy? And speaking of crazy, here's your first song, an old country classic—'Mama Tried,' by Merle Haggard. He turned twenty-one in prison and made his mama cry." I click off the mic. I'm flat.

"Not a lot of fire in your belly tonight." John looks concerned. "You sick?"

"Just ... my family." I really, really, really don't want it to matter. But it does.

He pats my arm. "Just be happy you have one."

"Whatever."

He glares and gestures at the mike. If I don't get the next song ready, I'll have dead air.

"So, Ugly Children, how about those parents? Like 'em or hate 'em? I can't decide these days. They take care of me, feed me, and let me sleep in their house, but they're seriously clueless, you know? Don't you ever just want to stand in front of them and yell, 'THIS IS ME—WHY DON'T YOU LIKE ME?' Is there a Bureau of Parents?

Can I get another set? But enough of that. We're here to focus on those lovely, kind, sweet women who are our mothers. Or at least someone else's mothers. How about a little Frank Zappa, something catchy but messed up? Here's 'My Guitar Wants to Kill Your Mama.'"

John looks like I slapped somebody.

"Yes, I'm crabby." I glare, and he doesn't say a word.

Songs go on and come off. I keep getting angry so John shuts off the mic, and eventually I give up and just play music.

I try one last time before everything's over. "Maybe, friends, our moms could remember their own crappy teenage lives. That would help. Back when they were stuck doing what someone else wanted them to do."

John's reaching for the mic to shut it off again, but I grab it. "Before I go, Ugly Children, your task for this show is to decorate the statue of our local founding father, Merriweather Maxfield, since he's also kind of the mother of our town. He's a uniparent! And he's bronze and pretty ugly, so he could use some sprucing up. Remember the side seam in his crotch? Make sure you restock the condoms, but see what else you can do to it. And thank you for the B side wall. It's … it's just … wow. Thank you. It's awesome." I can't say any more, and they'll probably paint over it after this show, but I have to thank them before it's gone. "I'm Gabe, this is Beautiful Music for Ugly Children on 90.3 KZUK, and for our benediction, here's 'Stacy's Mom' from Fountains of Wayne. She's the ultimate MILF. See you next week."

There really is a crevice in his crotch, like the one in

the front of tighty whiteys. People leave all sorts of things in that spot besides condoms. *We want an accurate historical picture*, the town bigwigs said, and this is what a Civil War uniform looked like when First Lieutenant Merriweather Maxfield came here to settle our fine community.

I probably sucked so bad they won't do it. I don't blame them.

Saturday noon. I check my email and see nothing, then decide to get on my bike and work off a little of the Pepsi spare tire. Plus, I'm curious to see if I sucked as bad as I thought I did. When I go by the Merriweather Maxfield statue, there's an entire bouquet sticking out of the side of the crotch of his pants, and "UCB!!" chalked all over him, including on his dick, or where I'd imagine his dick would be. Maybe Merriweather Maxfield is a trans man—maybe he has no dick. I take a couple photos with my phone, since I'm guessing someone will come by and fix it later. We don't want the town father to be defaced, after all.

Then I ride my ass all the way out to the B side wall, and the graffiti is still there. Amazingly. I take another picture, just in case, and I solemnly swear to be better next week.

I need them.

MICHAEL JACKSON IS THE NEW ELVIS SINCE THE WORLD WENT CRAZY WHEN EACH OF THEM DIED

Wednesday noon. I'm in the caf, drinking a Pepsi. Heather waves and smiles, and I try not to look too interested or desperate. Then Paige comes and sits with me, because she says I look sad. Less than two weeks left, she says. Even though I'm not sad, that news instantly makes me feel better.

Algebra, then study hall. I let my mind drift to the Vibe contest and radio songs, but it strays to Heather, and I feel a little bad. It's kind of like cheating on Paige, even though there's nothing to cheat on.

But letting myself think about a girl is new for me. Another B side track.

I imagine softness, sweet smells, pretty hair, pretty eyes,

and Heather's there, smiling that lovely smile, waving her lovely hand. Then Paige storms into my mind and starts yelling at me for thinking about some other girl. Imaginary Heather slinks away.

If anybody could ruin a fantasy, it would be Paige.

But it gives me an idea.

Thursday after school. "John, do you think we could do a show about…"

"Sex? Drugs? Rock and roll? All of the above?"

I gulp. "Well…sex. Maybe seduction?"

"Give me three seconds and I'll get you three hundred songs."

"Don't you think your lady friends would like it if you lasted longer than three seconds?"

"Watch your mouth, sonny." But he grins.

A new kind of conversation for us. I think John likes me as a guy.

I take the deepest breath I can.

"Good evening, and welcome to your sexy midnight hour. I'm Gabe, and this is Beautiful Music for Ugly Children, on community radio KZUK, 90.3. I hope you're with your sweetie, because this show is for anybody who wants to get it on." And then the smooth sounds of Marvin

Gaye float into the darkness. There's no question what Marvin wants.

When he's done seducing the world, I'm ready to go. "So, Ugly Children Brigade, are you into seduction this evening? I hope your lovely A sides are rubbing against other people's B sides, making sparks between you. And speaking of B sides, that wall is so crazy cool I still can't believe it. Thank you again for making it. Are you there right now? I hope so. For our next foray into seduction, let's try on 'Inside My Love,' Minnie Riperton, just for that slow friction."

Paige's face floats through my mind. Then Heather's.

The phone rings.

"KZUK, the Z that sucks."

"You aren't really doing this show, are you? Who the hell are you going to seduce?"

"Thanks for the support, BFF. Maybe Cher. Wouldn't you like to know?"

She's insulted, for real or for fake I can't tell. "You have to tell me! I'm the only friend you have."

"Not true. John's my friend." John gives me a thumbs-up while digging around in the crate marked *seduction songs*.

"You know what I mean. Back to the question: who are you trying to seduce?"

You, Paige. And if not you, maybe Heather. "Nobody in particular."

"You'd better tell me when you figure it out."

"What are you doing tonight, pray tell? Seducing Bobby X? Or reading a book?"

She snorts. "Wouldn't you like to know?"

"That means you're reading a book."

"My parasitology textbook is way more exciting than you are." She hangs up.

As the song ends, John hands me a CD and I get it into a player, looking at it just enough to know its name. "So, Ugly Children, maybe you're dancing. I've heard it's a good seduction technique. Here's Rihanna and her not-so-subtle sexual requests for her Rude Boy. Then we'll slow it down for some real dancing with Usher. And remember, if no one's around to dance with, a broom will do. And that's my request for tonight, since you all seem willing to do my bidding for some odd reason. Get those dancing brooms and mops and make a crowd near City Hall, by the fountain. I bet that's a lovely spot for tonight's midnight tryst."

Then I'm off the air, and John's giving me the eye. "Who was that on the phone?"

"Paige."

"Your smart friend?" He doesn't see her often, but he thinks she reads too much. Which she does.

"She's not that smart." I don't tell him she's got the third highest GPA in our class.

The phone rings again.

"KZUK, the Z that sucks. What do you want now?"

The voice at the other end is startled. "What do you mean, what do I want?" It's not Paige.

I'm caught completely off guard. "Uh ... "

Then the voice gets a little sexier. "I want to know who you're trying to seduce."

My brain has exploded. "Well … "

"Do you know who this is?"

"It's … "

"It's Mara! Who else would it be?" The bounce is back in her voice, but she pauses. "Maybe you have other girls who call you."

I try to sound macho. "Tonight you're the only one."

"That's not true, if you asked me what I wanted."

"I … "

"Would you like to hang out sometime?"

"Pardon me?" I'm not sure what she said. I think I know, but I need her to say it again.

"Would you like to meet me sometime for coffee?"

She's asking me out.

I've never been on a date in my life.

"How about the Hag?" She doesn't seem to sense my cluelessness.

The Coffee Hag is a very funky coffeehouse, very left-wing alternative. I can fit in there. Or at least not stick out. "The Hag is fine."

She sounds pleased. "How about next week?"

Do I really want to do this? Can I really pull it off? My brain ticks through a thousand thoughts in a second. Then I make my voice as low as possible. "Let's do it after graduation."

"Are you a senior?"

Shit shit shit. "No, but my cousin across town is, and I have to help with his reception." Not a bad save. Hopefully.

"Maybe the week after? Can I call you?"

"Sure." That gives me time to figure out what to wear. Or to chicken out, whichever comes first.

"Great! I'll be the one with the daisy on my bag."

She may be way too perky for me. But meeting someone as Gabe—that's exciting. And scarier than wearing a Mango into a men's room.

"I'll be the one with the red Chuck Taylors." Red shoes will make me seem manly—won't they?

"See you soon!"

I hang up and wonder what I've done.

It's all right, Gabe. You know it's all right.

Elvis could be completely full of shit.

No time to think. Dead air. "Still out there seducing each other? That's good, Ugly Children, that's good. Spread the love but wear a glove. How about a little Whitesnake? Hmm, is that a pun?" I give up before it gets any weirder.

John's eyeing me from the back of the studio, where the music crate ended up. "Paige again on the phone?"

"Nope."

"Another girl?"

"Yup."

"You're kidding!" He puffs up his chest. "My best record was fifteen in an hour. And women can be pretty vicious, you know. They'd line up outside the window of the studio and wave at me, then go to the pay phone to call me, then pull each others' hair and scratch each other and do it all over again. Good times, I tell you … good times." His face is dreamy as he remembers.

"I don't think I'll ever get to fifteen."

"So what did the other girl want?"

"To ask me out."

He can see my hesitation. "What's the problem?"

"When did you find out I'm a guy?"

"Three weeks ago? I don't know."

"So imagine what it's like to be asked out—as a guy—when I couldn't even tell *you* my secret, and I've known you forever. She thinks she's asking out a bio guy."

"What's a bio guy?"

"A biological guy."

"But what's the problem?"

"This is ME we're talking about. There are a thousand problems."

John pats my shoulder. "Women are just plain scary. Sometimes, though, you just gotta take the plunge. Test the waters." His southern twang is showing. "What's the worst thing that could happen?"

"If she has an older brother, he could bash my head in if she thinks I'm lying about being a guy. That's not usually a factor in other guy's dates."

"Well, your water probably has more sharks in it than most people's." He flings me a CD of Insane Clown Posse. "But what if the sharks are taking a nap and it's smooth sailing?"

There's a seduction song by Insane Clown Posse? "Throwing CDs isn't the best way to treat your music collection, is it?" I fling the CD back to him. "I'll try to imagine the sharks doing something else. Like listening to shark music."

"Do you think there's such a thing as shark music?

Maybe in the sixties, with surfer music and all that." He hands me the last CD and fixes me with a look. "Think positive. This song will bring the house down, by the way."

I glance at it, and he's right. Then I'm on. "For our last song this evening, here's 'Pour Some Sugar on Me' by Def Leppard. Just make sure to clean up your mess, Ugly Children. We don't want things all sticky." John is trying not to laugh out loud. "I'm Gabe, of course, awaiting your seduction. Like Elvis says, don't be cruel, and I'm back next week right here on KZUK, community radio, 90.3."

John claps. "You are amazing."

I feel like I've run ten miles.

And now I have a date. Obviously, pigs are flying somewhere, and Jesus will be back tomorrow.

We decide on a McDonald's trip after the show, before we check out the UCB's work. I order a cheeseburger Happy Meal because my stomach's still got Mara sharks in it, but John orders two Big Mac meals. Once we've got our goods, we drive around forever, to give them more time to finish things. Finally we drive by City Hall to see if there's anything there, and there are at least twenty mops and brooms propped up around the fountain, some in embraces made by rope arms tacked onto their bodies, some lying down on top of each other, getting it on in that mop-ly way. *UGLY CHILDREN BRIGADE—SEDUCED BY GABE* is chalked on the flat ledge around the fountain.

Is anybody going to come after me for vandalism? That's the last thing I need.

John's just staring. "What a piece of work. Look—that

one has an actual face." Someone's cut eyes, nose, ears, and a mouth out of felt and glued it to the broom. The mop that's making out with the broom has a face too.

"Look at that!" I point to a Swiffer WetJet in a tight embrace with a barn broom. "Mops and brooms fraternizing, heaven help us all."

John's got his phone out, snapping photos. "We should make a Facebook page for this stuff. Show everyone the work of the UCB."

"You're on Facebook?" Just when I think there can't be any more surprises in one night.

"Isn't everyone?"

When we finally get home, I let John out in his driveway. "Thanks for hanging out."

"You were awesome." He waves and goes into his house.

I get parked and head inside, but not before I hear very loud AC/DC coming through John's windows. Plenty of neighbors complain about the volume, and sometimes the cops come by, but they usually leave with smiles on their faces and CDs in their hands.

After I've brushed my teeth, I open my window and listen. Still AC/DC. I dust my Elvis 45 for a minute, admiring its label and its lack of scratches. If worst comes to worst, I could sell it and use that money to move away.

But I don't know if even that's worth selling my connection to John and Elvis. I need them too much.

As I'm drifting off to sleep, I consider telling Paige about my date, but I decide to keep it to myself. I don't need her crap if it doesn't work out.

ELVIS COSTELLO IS THE NEW ELVIS BECAUSE HE CHANGED HIS NAME TO HONOR THE KING

Monday. I check my email to see if there's an answer from the Vibe, and of course there's nothing. They must be having big yuks at their staff meetings: "Hey, did you see this girl who's a guy? What kind of stupid shit is that?" Every night, I listen for a while before I go to sleep. I imagine myself chatting, laughing, giving the promos, talking about concerts, playing commercials. Then I imagine going home to my apartment. Gabe's apartment.

Sometimes, when I open the door of that apartment, Paige is there on the couch, reading her textbooks and studying for med school. It's late at night, after my shift, and she's tired. We curl up on the couch for a while, and watch some TV, and then we...I can't even let myself go there. Too amazing. And it's too sad, because it will never happen, so why bother?

Tuesday: no email. Paige comes over, drags me to my room, and demands my laptop. "You absolutely have to see this." She pulls up Facebook and types in "Ugly Children Brigade." A page come up. Paige clicks on it, and it's a fan page, complete with an Ugly Children Brigade logo, photos, and 57 fans to go with it.

"No way." I click around to see if there's anyone I know. Paige is there, Heather Graves is there, and so is Mara, but I don't point that out to Paige. There are even some grown-ups: a local DJ who's not horrible, and Russ, the station manager of KZUK. "I'll have to tell John about this. Who made that logo?"

Paige is surprised. "John's on Facebook?"

"Evidently. Did you put this up?"

"Nope. I saw it on Allison's page."

I click through the photos. "Look—the wall, the mops, and check this out!" It's a photo of a movie marquee, one over by our local college. The letters have been rearranged to say *G BE R X—UGLY CH LDR N BRIG DE*. Must've been a vowel shortage. And there's a video of people setting up the mop display at City Hall. Paige and I fall over laughing when they set up the ones doing it by the fountain.

"So, are you going to 'like' them?" She sits back and looks at me.

"No." Liz has one friend on Facebook—Paige. Though I should probably friend John.

"How would anyone know that you're Gabe?"

"Look at my profile photo. It's a 45."

"So what? Change it—be Elvis or Donald Duck or Raggedy Ann. You're so dense you haven't said a word about the fact that people set up a Facebook fan page for your show!"

"There are Facebook fan pages for everything from farts to Jell-O." Which is true.

"You know what I mean." She points at the screen. "'Like' them."

Remembering *MITCH'S B SIDE = SATAN!* makes me open another window, log on, and change my profile pic to Elvis Costello, just to be less obvious. Then I 'like' the Ugly Children Brigade.

"See? That wasn't so hard." Paige is smug.

I don't say anything.

"Nothing's going to happen to you because you liked the UCB."

How does she know?

"Let's go to a movie, music boy. You need some fun in your life."

"There's fun in my life. There's my show, and John."

"And me." She whacks me with a copy of *Rolling Stone* that's sitting on my desk. "I mean real fun. Like regular people have fun."

"I don't have any money."

Another whack, for emphasis. "You can owe me, loser. Let's get out of here before you chicken out of anything else in your life."

While we're waiting for the movie to start, I focus on how lovely Paige's mouth is. She's got very luscious lips, and a beautiful smile. Sometimes I just have to stare.

The world is better as long as she's in it.

When I get home at midnight, way too late for a school night, Pete is sprawled out in the living room, watching *Deadliest Catch*. I can barely stand that show—all the waves and surf make me feel like I'm drowning. But I sit down anyway. There haven't been many bonding opportunities, so I'm gonna take it when I get it.

I clear my throat so he notices me. Nothing. He's pretty focused on the crab pots the guys are trying to tie down while the waves crash everywhere.

"Can't sleep?"

"Nope." He doesn't turn his head away from the TV. He's got school tomorrow, too—he's a junior—but he doesn't seem too worried about it. My mom would kill us both if she knew we were still up.

"Can I ask you a question?" I try to sound like I know what I'm asking.

"I guess."

"How do you know when a girl likes you?"

He actually looks at me. "You think I'm going to discuss that with you? That's just ... no way." The look on his face is almost—not quite, but almost—disgusted.

"I just thought ... you know ... " I don't even go on, because I feel so sad.

Silence. We watch the guys flail around for a while, and my feet get cold just thinking about how frigid that water is.

Then a quiet voice: "You like girls?"

"I, uh ... yeah."

He keeps watching TV. "You know they like you when they smile a lot. It's a dead giveaway."

More silence. But I'll take it.

Finally all the fish are fished and the guys are happy happy, big grins all around. The seawater smashing everywhere makes my stomach flip around.

He chances a glance. "Did you know the production crew has to throw away their cameras after every season? All the ice and salt and crap wears them out."

"I had no idea."

"What do you think Mom and Dad would do if I went to Alaska and tried out for a spot on a crew?" There's a little flicker of a grin. "Sounds better than college."

"Yup."

We watch a few more minutes, then Pete switches it to VH1. "It was almost over anyway." There's a rerun of *Flavor of Love*.

"A little dose of Flav?" Now Pete's a little more like the brother he was before the B side started playing.

"Don't you wonder how Chuck D put up with him?" They were both in Public Enemy way back when. The show is so obnoxious we can't stop laughing, and by the time an hour's gone by, it feels better between us.

I'll watch as much TV with him as he wants me to. Even *Scary Ice Cold Fishing*.

HARRY POTTER IS THE NEW ELVIS BECAUSE THEY'RE BOTH MAGIC

Friday afternoon. I go to John's to get some music but also just to hang out. Paige is with Bobby X. Boring. And they don't want me around anyway.

When John opens the door, he's beaming. "I was hoping you'd come by. Got a surprise for you. Consider it a graduation gift." Graduation is next week. John tries to look mysterious, but mostly he looks goofy as he brings me a slip of paper. It's got a name and a phone number on it. "Want a job at a music store?"

"You're kidding." My parents will flip if it's true.

John's got his hands on his hips. "If you've got this big new plan for a new life, saving money would help. You know Professor McSwingy's?"

"How'd anybody ever come up with that name?"

"Ask Chris sometime. He's the guy who runs McSwingy's and he needs someone for evenings, so I told him I have a friend who knows about music. It's not guaranteed, but I'm pretty sure it's yours if you want it."

I love Professor McSwingy's. It's very vintage in its approach to music, which is to say you can go there and find almost any recording from any musician from the last half of the twentieth century, not to mention stuff from this century. Plus, high school kids don't go there—it's not hip like the Best Buy in the mall, ha ha.

"Did you … um … tell him about me?"

John rolls his eyes. "He won't care if you're a potbellied pig as long as you know music."

"It can't be this easy."

"Why not?"

"My parents bitch me out for not having a job, and one falls into my lap? No way." Then reality crashes in. "If people stare at me instead of buying Radiohead CDs, there's no way I can do it."

He moves toward the phone. "I'll call him and tell him I lied about that friend."

"Don't you dare!" I can't bear to think about this kind of job slipping through my fingers. It's too perfect.

He dials anyway. "How about I call him and tell him you're coming by?" Then someone answers. "Hi, it's John. I'm sending over my friend right now—do you have time? Good. Thanks." He hangs up and grins at me. "He's a bigger music dork than you are."

"Yeah, but who'd I learn it from?"

He waves me away. "You're welcome. Now scram."

I owe him. Whenever he's sick, I bring him my mom's soup, and I mow his lawn sometimes. But a radio show and a job are bigger than that.

Professor McSwingy's is in a little storefront in the older part of town, close to one of the pawnshops and the Coffee Hag. The bell above the door announces my presence. Promo posters and album flats are all over the walls and windows, and not just Kanye West or Jay-Z but people like the Clash, Steely Dan, early Bruce Springsteen. All sorts of old gold. I walk to the counter and see a list by the cash register titled *THE BEST BAND NAMES IN THE WORLD*, with five names: Trulio Disgracias, The Sacred Heart of Elvis, The Garden Hos, Honest Bob and the Factory to Dealer Incentives, and Quiet Time and the Whisper Kids.

Chris is an older version of Beck—tall and stringy, with hair to match. "You John's friend?"

"His neighbor." My voice is too high, so I pull it down. "And friend."

"You interested in working nights? It'd be three or four nights a week, depending on what I need."

"Sure." It comes out better this time.

"What's your name?"

I open my mouth. Shut it. Open it again. "Gabe."

Chris checks me out again, which I expected. He's been doing it since I came in. I know sometimes people read me as a girl, but I really want him to believe my name is Gabe.

He finally looks at my face again. "Who's your favorite artist of all time?"

My mind flips through album covers. "No way to pick just one. Stevie Wonder. Adele, if she's not too mopey. David Byrne. Lyle Lovett. Sharon Jones and the Dap-Kings."

"Odd combo." Chris gives me another serious look. "Top five one-hit wonders."

John wasn't kidding—total music dork. "Number one: 'Hot Pants' by Salvage."

"It's the Holy Grail." He nods, very solemnly, impressed that I know my stuff. "What else?"

Now I've got them lined up in my head. "'Relax,' Frankie Goes to Hollywood. 'Vehicle,' Ides of March. 'Rapper's Delight,' Sugar Hill Gang, and 'Whip It,' Devo."

"No way is 'Whip It' a one-hit wonder." Chris's face is very serious.

"Devo never had another Top 40 hit, so it qualifies." I'm smug in my righteousness.

"You like Devo?"

"I love Devo." My hand is on my heart, so he knows I'm serious.

"When can you start?" He walks toward a door at the back of the store. "Let's do the paperwork."

"What?" The word squeaks out.

He notices I've stopped walking. "W-2s and all that?" He gives me a little wave to follow him.

In the back room, there's a desk surrounded by stacks and stacks of boxes and paper, with one chair in front of the desk and one behind. Three enormous mounds of promotional posters and displays are behind the desk, and the rest of the room is full of CDs, albums, and cassettes.

Chris takes the chair behind the desk and digs in a drawer to find the forms. I sit in front and bite my nails. Cliché, but I can't figure out what else to do. It's choice time.

He slides the forms across the desk—a basic application and a W-2. I print slowly so my hand doesn't shake. "Gabe Williams" goes in the blank for my name. There's a spot at the bottom to list my favorite musical artists, so I put down Britney Spears, just to see what he'll say. On the W-2 I put down Elizabeth Mary Williams and my social security number, then push the forms back over.

He reads the app and scowls, then stands up and sticks out his hand. "I can't give you a job. Thanks for coming in."

I stand up and shake his hand quick, head bowed low. "Thanks for the interview."

His face is pained. "How can you love Stevie and her, too? I keep the Britney CDs behind a Tool display so I don't have to see her." The look on my face must say it all, and he laughs at me. "You weren't serious?"

"Uh … no. You already asked me my favorites, remember? Devo, David Byrne?"

His face clears. "Right. Chalk it up to too many drugs. You start tomorrow." We shake hands for real this time.

But I can't leave without asking. "Did you read the W-2?" Elvis, be with me. Let it be all right.

Chris glances down at the form, pauses, then looks at me. "What you call yourself is no business of mine, as long as I can legally pay you with this social security number. Do you want to know your hourly wage?"

My heart slows down a little. Elvis, you helped. "Sure." I'd do this job for free, so the money's a bonus.

"It's $8.50 an hour, plus a store discount of 30 percent."

"Damn!" I'll have no paycheck because I'll put it all back into the store, but that's okay.

He looks dismayed. "That's not all right?"

"That's great! Thank you!" We shake again. "What time do you want me?"

"Come by at four, and we'll go over stuff. We close at nine, so four to nine will be your normal shift. After school gets out, I'll give you more hours. I'll stay with you tomorrow night so I'm sure you've got it all. Have you ever run a register?"

"No. Is that bad?"

Chris claps me on the back. "Easy enough to teach you. Don't trip on the boxes on your way out. This room's a mess." He leads the way back into the store. "Maybe you can straighten it up sometime."

"See you tomorrow." I turn around to walk out, but turn back. "Do you have any other employees?"

"It's just me right now." He shakes my hand one more time. "Tomorrow at four."

"See you then." He goes back behind the counter to help a customer. I really want to skip to my car, but skipping is not manly.

My parents are so pleased about my job, they decide we should go out to celebrate the event, plus it's Friday and nobody wants to cook. Paige and John come too. Things seem about 2 percent less tense, and nobody asks what name I'm using at McSwingy's. After supper, John goes home, tipping me a wink since I'll see him later, then Paige and I go buy Oreos and eat the entire package in her back yard. Then we almost heave because we haven't done that in a long time and we're out of practice.

When I leave, she pouts a little. "When are you going to take me to the station?" She knows John goes with me every week.

"Are you in a hurry?"

"No, but ... I just want to go." She gives me a quick hug and I want to hold on longer, but I don't.

"You promise, right?" She pulls back and points at me.

"I promise."

Paige smiles, and that luscious mouth works its magic on me. I'm glad it's getting dark, because I don't want her to see me blush.

Before I get John so we can go to the station, I check my email, hoping for something from the Vibe. Even a no would be better than all this stupid-ass waiting.

Nothing.

My show tonight is about guitar solos—dumb, but it works all right. Some of it is heavy metal hair-band bullshit, of course, but it's still useful for getting out the jams, and I'm not above an air guitar solo or two. I manage to plug in some Zeppelin and Pink Floyd, so that's worth it. My chatter is good, too. Or better, at least.

I don't say anything about the job. But the nice Facebook page deserves a mention.

"All right, Ugly Children Brigade, I found your Facebook fan page, and wow. Just wow. I still don't understand why you do it, but you rock, ha ha I made a pun, and talking to you is the best part of my week. And I think you'll like tonight's task. Ready? Find as many garden creatures as you can—gnomes especially—and create a party for them somewhere in town. Just make sure you put everyone back in their gardens when you're finished taking pictures, all right? No stealing."

John likes heavy metal, so he plays some pretty impressive air guitar. I find his hair-band appreciation very strange, considering his age, but whatever turns your turntable.

Saturday afternoon at 3:45. I can barely drive to McSwingy's.

I've done everything I can to make sure I look good. But what if I look like a freak? What if I've always looked like a freak? Wouldn't Paige have told me? I think about going home and trying again, but if I do, I'll be late.

What if people laugh at me?

As I walk up to the front door, I discreetly check out my clothes in the window. They don't say "girl." They say "this person needs a better wardrobe." And that's true.

It's daytime, and I'm not just a voice. Welcome, ladies and gentlemen, to Gabe's first truly public performance.

When I walk in, the bell above the door jingles and Chris looks up. "Gabe! Hey! Ready to learn the ropes?"

I nod.

He chuckles after he looks at my face. "Please don't crap your pants if a customer talks to you. It's not that scary." He can see I don't believe him. "Seriously. It's okay."

I swallow. "Then let's go."

Chris hands me a nametag that says *GABE*. "Pin this on, and I'll show you around."

It's a piece of my future, right here in my hand. The future is now. The tears are close, so I blink fast. There's no way I can cry right now.

"You all right?"

"Yup. Right behind you." I pin the nametag on and take a deep breath. Now or never. *Right, Elvis?*

The job is easy. The register pretty much does what you tell it to do, and how hard is it to stack up CDs in a spot on a rack? Chris and I talk music—he used to be a roadie for the Replacements—and I tell him about John and his enormous collection. He shows me all the different stacks of LPs and 45s in the back, and we talk about a plan to sell them cheap. Then he shows me how to clean the bathroom, which will also be my job. Gross. But it's a small price to pay.

I also talk to four people. That's not a lot, but it's still four more who can put the name Gabe to my face. Three of them barely look at me, which is fine, because I barely look at them. The fourth one is stoned, and he keeps trying to stare deeply into my eyes, so I just play along while I help him find his Bob Marley CDs. Every so often he says, "Whoa." I just say, "Damn straight." By tomorrow he'll think I'm a hallucination.

Suddenly it's nine p.m. I'm tired, but I'm not. I could do this job for twenty-four hours straight.

"Feel okay about it?" Chris makes sure the front door is locked and he shuts off the lights. Then he takes me out the back door.

"I'm solid."

Chris locks the final lock on the back door, then turns to me. "You did well, Gabe. Thanks for a good night."

"No, thank you! Really! You … um … yeah. Thanks." It takes a second to get the gushing under control.

"See you on Monday, all right? Then we'll talk about what nights you can work next week. The nights will vary, but we'll schedule around whatever else you need to do."

"Sure thing."

He turns to walk away, but not before he gives me a salute. I give him one back, then walk around the corner to where my car is parked.

I just laid down another B side groove.

It really, really, really isn't manly, so I look to see if anyone's watching. But there's no one, so I do it. I skip the final fifty yards to my car.

I'm in a club now. The guys-who-work-in-a-record-store club. And the words "record store" are really important. But the best word is "guys."

On Sunday morning, the garden creature party is staring me in the face from the front page of the *Maxfield Courier*.

It says "submitted photo" underneath it, which means the Ugly Children didn't call some *Courier* photographer to document it. The caption says, *Garden creatures of all kinds have a party at Food Pride on Friday evening.*

"Garden creatures of all kinds" means gnomes, giraffes, angels, one lawn jockey, a few Madonnas, a couple Buddhas, and some squirrels. All of them are positioned in front of the doors of the store. Some are talking to each other, some are set so they look like they're pushing carts, and others look like they're dragging grocery bags out of the store.

My dad, who's sitting at the table and having breakfast, laughs out loud. "Look at this. There are some strange kids out there, to think that up."

"Yeah, guess so." I can't say any more or I'll lose it. The sweat is pouring off me. Finally he leaves, so I sneak the paper off the table.

When I get it upstairs, I cut out the photo of the garden party and stash it in a desk drawer along with the rest of the paper. I'll smuggle the remains over to John's, so nobody says, "Hey, why is there a hole in this paper?" when they're putting it out for the recycle people. I'm not ready to confess. This show belongs to me, John, and the UCB.

I drive to Food Pride, but everything's gone, so at least they listened to my request to put stuff back. One scruffy squirrel got left on top of a pile of softener salt, and he looks lonely up there, so I take him home and put him with my mom's gnome back by the fountain. They can plan the next garden party.

JUSTIN BIEBER IS THE NEW ELVIS ONLY SHORTER AND A LOT MORE ANNOYING

Tuesday at five p.m., and it's finally graduation. I've never been so bored in my life. With 350 kids in your class, it takes forever, even though they run us through like cattle.

The guy in front of me is Paul Willard. When we lined up to march in, he sort of smiled. I sort of smiled back. We said a couple things. That was enough.

Then I hear Mr. Taylor, the principal, say it: "Elizabeth Mary Williams." I smile, walk up the stairs, grab the diploma, shake hands, walk down the stairs on the other side, repeat the smile/shake hands at the bottom of the stairs, and go sit down, praying that Mara isn't here to see me attached to that name.

If I have my way, Mr. Taylor's announcement was the

last public pronunciation of the words "Elizabeth Mary Williams."

Finally we can go home for some cake. I didn't get my way about no party, so some of my parents' friends come by and drop off gifts. Hopefully it's not stupid stuff—what I want is cash and gift cards. I smile and act polite for as long as I can, but then I go upstairs and change.

"Where are you going?" Mom's sitting at the table, eating more cake with Dad. Everybody's gone.

"Graduation party. Gonna pick up Paige."

She pats the chair. "Come sit down." She looks at my dad, and he nods.

"Uh ... no thanks." I'm not really in the mood for family togetherness.

"We have a gift for you, and you can't have it unless you sit."

I sit. What if it's something good?

My dad clears his throat and glances at me. "We didn't know ... what was appropriate ... "

"Joe, this isn't the time for a speech." My mom touches his hand.

He reaches into his breast pocket and pulls out an envelope, which he hands to me while looking at my mom. "Take a trip. You and Paige. Or buy a box of vintage albums, we don't care."

I take the envelope and open it to find twenty-dollar bills. A lot of them. "Not to be rude, but should I count it?" I thumb through the money. "There's five hundred dollars in here."

Mom smiles, but not at me. "Or something to take with you to college. Orientation must be coming up soon." She wants me to throw her a bone.

"I'll let you know, I promise." I can't stand her face, sort of desperate and sad and happy all at the same time while she stares at the table. "Again, not to be rude, but can I go now? Paige is waiting for me."

My dad swallows his cake. "Don't drink, and be home before I go to work tomorrow morning."

"No problem." I head up the stairs and shove my envelope of money into a dresser drawer. Then I book out the door before we have to have more conversations while they don't look at me.

Bank, here I come. It's savings account time.

I pick up Paige, and she directs us to this enormous party on someone's farm. There are bunches of cars parked in the driveway, which must be a mile long, and more cars on the main road. We each grab a beer from the keg, and I make a mental note to remember what Paige is wearing so I can find her later. She'll have to be scraped off the ground, I'm sure, and poured back in the car. I wonder where Bobby X is.

Paige wanders around like she's the hostess, flirting with any guy she can and moving through all the different circles of people she knows, like she's in demand. I follow her around, but people don't see me because they can't take their eyes off of her.

"Liz?"

I turn around, and it's Heather Graves.

Pull the voice low. "Hey, uh, Heather." If I had a dick, and I don't mean a Mango, it would be hard right now. She's a goddess: long flowing hair, lots of cleavage, and tight shorts. The imaginary words on her forehead are *DO ME*. My heart rate goes up to a zillion.

"Are you having fun?" She smiles at me like she really wants me to answer that question.

"It's better than sitting around with my folks."

"Are you with someone?" It almost sounds like that question has a suggestion behind it. Then again, I may be hearing things.

"I'm following Paige around." I gesture to where Paige is standing in a circle of six guys, tossing her hair like someone's filming her.

"She does like her followers, doesn't she?"

I throw the snark ball back to her. "We've been friends since kindergarten."

"Oh." Heather clears her throat. "What are you doing in the fall? I'm going to the U of M, for business. Are you going to school?"

"Not in the fall. But I can't imagine myself working at McSwingy's forever."

"You work at McSwingy's?" Her face brightens. "I love that place!"

Then I realize what I've done: I work there as Gabe, not Liz.

I can run away now, or I can keep going.

I let my feet decide, and they don't move—from fear

or from a desire to keep talking to a goddess, I don't know. So I take a deep breath. "I just started."

"I can spend hours in there. Do you guys have the latest Justin Timberlake?"

"Mr. Dick in a Box? Sure, we've got it." At least I hope we have it.

Her smile is bright in the semi-darkness. "When do you work next? I'll come down and get it."

"Uh..." Think, Gabe. "I'm not sure. I'll be there a lot now that school's done." I remind myself to smile back. She's sucking all the thoughts out of my head.

"Well, I'm sure I'll see you." Heather gives me a potentially flirty look. "I'm sorry we didn't get to know each other at school. Can I have your number?"

The planet must be exploding tomorrow, because only at the end of time could I imagine Heather Graves asking for my number. But I give it to her and she puts it in her phone.

"Thanks." She smiles while she looks me up and down. "And you sure the hell are cute."

"I'm not who you think..."

"Whoever you are, you're plenty." Her grin is more than slightly suggestive.

All I can do is blink. "I... uh..."

She leans in close. "You're adorable." Her lips are so close to mine... so very, very close and luscious. I'm cheating on Paige's lips. Maybe even all of her.

Then she backs away. "See you at McSwingy's." She

doesn't seem surprised that I'm completely incapable of making a sound. She turns around and walks away.

It's time to go. My heart can't take another conversation like that.

But if I'm really going to leave, I have to find Paige, and that's hard. I search through each little clump of people, but I hear no bubbly voice attached to a head tossing its hair. Finally I find her sitting on the edge of a hay bale, working the drama queen angle. She's got on purple flip-flops with cute black ribbons—decorated especially for tonight, she said—so while she talks she bounces her foot to show off her shoes.

A guy in her crowd says, "Hey, have you heard that radio show? Beautiful Children and Ugly Music or something like that?"

Paige turns to him. "It's Beautiful Music for Ugly Children, and—"

I grab her arm. "I'm out of here."

"What?" Paige pulls her arm back and glares.

"Get a ride home with someone else." I move out of her circle. Before I get too far, I hear one guy say, "Is she in our class?" Then someone else says, "Yeah, you know, that lesbo chick." If I went and found Heather, she could show them who the real lesbo chick is. Or maybe she's bi.

Finding the car is almost impossible in the dark. I'm unlocking the door and I hear Paige.

"Gabe! Shit, I mean Liz! Liz!" She's racing down the driveway, somehow managing not to run out of her flip-flops. "You can't leave!"

"I told you I was going."

"But I'm having fun!"

"I can't … the show … you outed me back there … I can't. I need to go." I open my car door, which is hard because my hands are shaking and I'm mad at myself for being such a chicken. "Get in."

She stomps her foot. "I did not! They don't know it's your show. But they should. You need to lighten up!" I can practically see the pink and purple ribbons trailing after her in the dark, just like that stubborn kindergarten girl.

"Really? Have you ever had two identities?"

"No, but name it and claim it, just like you told the UCB."

"Yeah, but … "

"You're Gabe now. Liz was high school. Get your ass back to the party." She stomps up the driveway with no backward glance.

I start the car and fiddle with the radio, willing my hands to stop trembling. The only stations I can find are country, classic rock, Christian sermons, and polka. Only in Minnesota is there polka on the radio. I listen to twenty minutes of it. It's not horrible.

I hate it when she's right.

I go back up the driveway, get another beer so I have something to hold, then sit down on a hay bale to figure out a show about radio songs, just in case the Vibe email arrives. Then I ponder when the Mango's going to get here. Nobody talks to me, but I don't talk to anyone either.

I see Heather Graves again, hanging on to Paul Willard,

and she waves, which he doesn't see. You never suspect it of the pretty girls, which makes it even more hilarious when they prove you wrong.

Paige floats by again in the middle of a crowd. While I watch her, I think about how confident she is. I want some of that.

What would Elvis do in this situation?

I'd walk right up, smile big, and join in the party.

He's never said that before.

I mentally step out of myself and stand about ten feet in front of my hay bale. There's a basic-looking but slightly feminine guy sitting there. He's kind of cute, and he looks like he wants to have a good time, but he also looks like he's afraid someone will spit on him. Or worse. He's actually kind of pathetic—eager, but sad and scared at the same time.

Dammit.

So I take Elvis's advice. I join Paige in her latest circle, finishing my beer while I listen and occasionally talk to people. By three a.m., ten people have asked if I graduated tonight and if I'm really in this class. I've also heard five other people talk about my show, and I've caught Heather staring at me at least three times, though Paul caught her the second time. The last time she blew me an air kiss, which is permanently burned in my retinas.

This week is a show for graduation: freedom songs. My freedom. Graduation was one more track on my B side.

"Good early, early morning, folks, and welcome to Beautiful Music for Ugly Children here on community radio 90.3, KZUK. I'm Gabe, of course, and let's start our midnight hour with John Cougar Mellencamp's 'I Need A Lover (Who Won't Drive Me Crazy).' Sounds like freedom to me."

John's in the corner, hooting it up. "Everybody needs a lover like that."

"Dude, I'd just like a lover."

"Have you picked a task for the Ugly Children Brigade?"

I dig through the CDs, finding the next piece I want. "Not yet. Got any ideas?"

"Let me think while I smoke." He goes outside, taking my *ELVIS LIVES* Zippo with him, while I find the next song.

"So, Ugly Children, how's your night? How's your life? What's freedom to you? Being able to say the F-bomb any time you want? Or looking like a London punk with safety pins in your ears and a six-inch pink Mohawk? Or is it the freedom to think as you'd like, or be what you'd like? For some of you, maybe a fast car is freedom. Graduation is freedom, too—happy graduation to all those Maxwell East and Maxwell West seniors. Here's a fantastic example of American freedom, from Jimi Hendrix."

Then the sketchy CD player wonks out. Maybe it doesn't like me, or maybe it's just a piece of shit, but I jab and jab my finger at the PLAY button until it finally starts. Then it's "The Star-Spangled Banner," fat and loud in the night air. Only in our crazy country would someone think to play the national anthem on the electric guitar.

I'm ready when Hendrix is over, with the Boss in the place where Mellencamp used to be. "All right, late-night listeners, this show is a celebration of liberation, so let's hear the ultimate freedom song from Bruce Springsteen, right here on KZUK, community radio 90.3. You can't mistake this song for any other, I promise you, so let's go." Then "Born to Run" blasts onto the airwaves, and anything seems possible.

When it's done, I take the plunge again. "Music is freedom, too, and that's what I like about it: it makes people think in new ways. 'Born to Run' might make you hop in your car or on your motorcycle and get the hell out of town for a while. And if you can't do it, you at least think about it. Or maybe you book a vacation to the Grand Canyon. But if you can't do that, maybe you go outside and run around the block and knock over your neighbor, since she's out jogging with a friend, and you and the friend hit it off and get married a week later. All those new possibilities because of 'Born to Run.' How about a little more freedom, courtesy of motorcycles and old movies? Here's Steppenwolf's 'Born to Be Wild,' made famous by the film *Easy Rider*. Get going, friends. The open road's waiting for you."

John gives me a thumbs-up. "I showed you that movie."

Then the phone rings. I jump a foot, but grab it fast. "KZUK, the Z that sucks."

"Can we get coffee now? It's after graduation."

"Mara?" I should have expected her call, but I'm still surprised. My hands get clammy.

"I feel like I'm meeting a celebrity or something." She sounds like she's twelve.

"Trust me, I'm not that special."

"Let me be the judge of that."

I'm so glad she can't see me blush.

She keeps going. "How about this next Wednesday?"

I tick through my life, but I don't have to work, and when do I ever have any social stuff planned? "Okay by me."

"Did you see the paper last week? That was my picture of the garden party!"

"Sure did. I even cut it out." I feel like a dork admitting it. But right now I'm letting myself love the fact that a girl thinks I'm cool.

"I did too." I hear the smile in her voice. "What's the plan for the UCB tonight?"

"I'll let you know in a minute." Tonight I want them to decorate a stranger's car—not in a bad way, just a festive way. Balloons or streamers or flowers, something like that.

"I'm sure it's awesome, whatever it is." The smile in her voice is still there.

My mind is swept up in imagining Mara and me, talking and laughing and looking like some fluffy coffee commercial. Then I realize there's no music, just silence.

"Oh shit!" Mercifully, when I hit the button, Devo's "Freedom of Choice" slides onto the air.

Laughter from her end.

"Mara?"

More giggles. "The 'oh shit' went out on the air, too."

"WHAT?" I might puke.

"Just an added bonus for the Ugly Children Brigade."

I try to get myself together, but it's not working. Best choice: get off the phone. "Wednesday, seven, Coffee Hag, see you then."

"'Bye." She's still chuckling when she hangs up.

Who knows if the FCC has mobile trucks just waiting to bust people who use profanity on the air? I can't imagine they do, but you never know. I slow my breathing down.

John's back, and he's almost falling down. "Oh my heavens, OH my heavens ... thank god they have speakers in the hall. That was priceless." He keeps laughing as I get Akon's "Freedom" on its way.

"Yeah, thanks for your support."

His snorts are dying down. "It happens to everyone once or twice. Not a big deal." He looks into the crate of CDs. "How many more songs do you have left? What time is it?"

"Ten to one, and I have three more songs."

"I'm going for another smoke and a Pepsi." And he leaves again.

When the show is over and we're walking to the car, I realize my mistake. "John, I forgot to tell the UCB to decorate cars!"

"They'll figure out something. They're pretty creative."

When I get home, I check my email, just for fun. And there's one from the Vibe.

I stare at my pathetic inbox. One email. This one.

I don't want to know. But then I give in and click on it, because I can't *not* know.

While it opens up, I close my eyes and say a little prayer: *Dear Universe, please make this moment not suck completely. Thank you.*

When I open my eyes, I read very, very carefully.

Dear Gabriel:

We're glad to know you'd like to participate in our Summer Mondays in the Cities competition. We're confident our guest spot at the Vibe will be filled by a wonderful DJ, thanks to you and your fellow contestants. We will also change your name in our records.

We look forward to seeing you on July 12. Start planning your set—and don't forget your secret song!

Yours truly,
Thad Rosenbloom, Station Manager,
The Vibe 89.1

I print it off and run out the front door, banging it loud enough that I'll hear about it tomorrow morning, I'm sure. Then I pound on John's door. "They'll let me do it! Open up! You gotta see this!"

Finally the door opens, and John's standing there in a rumpled bathrobe. He doesn't look thrilled to see me. "Make it snappy."

"You're already in bed?"

"I know it's strange, but I'm tired. Make it snappy."

"The Vibe. They said I could compete as Gabe. Read." I shove the paper into his hand.

As he reads, his grin gets wider by the second. "I knew they'd take you. Congratulations!" He grabs me and hugs me, rough, like a man would hug a man. Neither of us are the hugging type. "We'll start work tomorrow. But now you gotta go." The Southern accent is sliding in.

"I'm gone. Go back to sleep." He shuts the door and I practically float back to my house. *July 12. July 12. July 12.* It's engraved on my brain.

Guest spot, here I come. As soon as I get back to my room, I turn on the Vibe and start writing down every song they play. I haven't done that before. Then I write a list of possible secret songs, and it's two pages long.

At 2:30, I put the pen down, turn off the radio, and try to crash. Right. About 3:30, I get up and dust my 45. Maybe Elvis really does know the truth, and it really is all right. Or maybe he's full of shit. Either way, things are all right for this minute, and that's fine with me.

As I'm drifting off, I hear a faint comment: *Do you doubt me?*

Elvis sounds testy.

The next morning I check the UCB's fan page, hoping they'll post pictures of whatever adventure they took themselves on. Of course it's magnificent: the words *OH SHIT* are chalked about a hundred times over the face of both Maxfield East and Maxfield West, covering the front of each school. Down at the bottom of the front wall, on each school, it says *HAPPY FREEDOM, SENIORS!*

I print off the pictures, then rummage around in a hall closet. When I find an empty photo album, I put last night's *OH SHIT* photos in there and write the date on them. On another page I put the pictures of the mops and brooms, then move that page ahead of the *OH SHIT* pictures so everything's in order. I find the clipping of the garden party at the grocery store and tuck it in the book, too.

God, I'm strange. But I can't help it. They make me feel like a rock star. Like I have something decent to say.

They make me feel like I matter.

KATY PERRY IS THE NEW ELVIS BECAUSE SHE LIKES KISSING GIRLS, TOO

Wednesday evening. When I get to the Coffee Hag, I sit by the wall so I can see both doors. I made sure to bind my chest extra-tight and iron my shirt, just for that put-together look. My hair is carefully combed, of course, and I chose glasses today for that studious look. James Franco, right? Normally it takes me about forty-five minutes to be sure I'm guy-ish enough—binder, clothes, shoes, hair, checked over and over and over again—but tonight it was ninety. I can't believe I'm doing this. I feel good, but I feel like I'm going to explode. With fear or excitement, I don't know.

I think about leaving, and I actually stand up. But I sit back down and stick my red feet out from under the table. The casual look is a little more convincing. I should lean back, put my arms behind my head, and put my crotch front and center just like bio guys do, but I couldn't be that macho if I channeled John Wayne.

Mara comes in, a big white daisy pinned to her book bag. She looks light, almost wispy, like the air could carry her away. I never noticed it at school. She's Björk without the swan dress, if Björk was about seventeen. I let her order coffee. When she turns around, mug in hand and licking the froth, I stand up and smile.

"Mara?"

"Gabe!" She brings her coffee mug away from her face, and I see a spot of foam on her lip. Sexy. She licks it off without a thought. Or maybe she's a tease. How the hell am I supposed to know? If she had imaginary words on her forehead, they would say *SCARY DUMB IDEA.*

I remind myself to push my voice into my chest. "I have a table over here."

"Great! Did you get a coffee?"

I pull out her chair for her. Nothing like chivalry to convince people you're a guy. "I did. I've been here a while."

"You have?" She looks concerned. "Am I late?"

"I like hanging out here. I brought a book." I point to my book bag at my feet.

"I've never seen you here before." She frowns a little. "And I usually come once a week."

"I mostly come in the morning, on weekends. I'm a morning person." Like any eighteen-year-old guy is a morning person.

"Oh. What's your favorite kind of coffee?" She smiles

again. I like that smile. It's serious, which is strange, since I thought she was perky. Her smile is gorgeous.

"Um ... I like mocha frappes."

"So why aren't you drinking one?" She gestures to the coffee mug. Definitely not a frappe glass.

"I like to switch it up." Please let her stop asking questions.

She sits in the chair opposite mine and looks at me. Frowns at me, in fact. "Do I know you from somewhere?"

My heart falls onto my Chucks. Maybe she really was at graduation. "How would we know each other?" I keep the smile light and the voice low. No panic.

"What church do you go to?"

"My family is a bunch of pagan tree worshippers." Oh man, not religion. The coffee discussion is hard enough.

The frown is still there. "Maybe it's not church. I'll think of it."

If all else fails, change the subject. "So, why did you start listening to KZUK?"

"My parents like it, so I grew up with it. Are you in high school?" She's frowning at me again.

I ignore the question. "KZUK's unique, that's for sure." Der, der, der—my brain's got a skip. Why the hell did I say that? I fiddle with my mug.

"How'd you get a show there?" She sips her coffee again. There's more foam on her lip, and she licks it off without a thought.

"KZUK will give anyone with a pulse some air time."

"Seriously, where do you go to school? West or East?" She's not giving this one up.

"New Sibley Day School." It's in the next town over.

"Really? My cousin goes to school there—Megan Anderson? I'll have to ask her if she knows you."

It figures.

"So what's on your iPod?" Mara pulls hers out of her bag, and it's attached to these funky, noise-damping headphones. She and her iPod mean business.

"Nothing too interesting." Which isn't true, but I don't want to bore her.

Fiddle fiddle. "I have 850 songs on here, and I want more. Isn't that stupid?"

I gesture to the moving pink rectangle. "Who's on it?"

"Everyone from Coldplay to Mozart." She sighs. "Sometimes I feel like I've heard it all already."

I think for a second. "Have you tried Brother Ali?"

"No."

"There you go."

Mara laughs. "You know what I mean. Right now I'm into nineties stuff, Nirvana and Blind Melon and the Dave Matthews Band..."

Her lips are red and shiny. Almost like Paige's. I'm cheating on Paige's mouth by looking at Mara's mouth. But I also cheated by looking at Heather's mouth, and the rest of her.

"Gabe?"

Caught. "Hmm?" I try not to look like I've been drifting.

"Are you listening?"

"Sure. Nirvana."

"You zoned out." She gives me a pouty face.

"I was … enjoying the view." I should just shut up.

Mara gathers up her iPod and stashes it away, and I see the blush creeping up her face. When she looks up again, she's frowning. "I just can't place you. Do you have a sister?"

My heart is under my Chucks. Hopefully all the color in my face is still there. "Nope, no sister, or cousin."

"It's not important. But you really do look familiar."

The panic rises, and I have to get out of here, like now, or my heart will leap out of my chest. I give her one more smile. "They say everyone has a twin."

I never should have agreed to this. This is such a small town, even with 40,000 people in it.

"Maybe so. Hey, do you want more coffee?" Mara stands up, foamed-up mug in her hand.

"Um, no thanks. I've gotta go."

She looks disappointed. "So soon?"

I try for casual. "I know. I'm sorry."

"Can we do it again?"

"Give me another call at the station."

"Sure. It's awesome to meet you."

"You too."

Mara moves to hug me, which is the worst idea I've imagined in a long time. I grab the coffee mug in her right hand and give it a couple hard shakes while I reach for my book bag. The mug is better than her hand, since mine is slimy with sweat. Then I bolt.

"Gabe!"

I focus on the door and get the hell out. The car's close, and I collapse when I get inside it.

It's all right, Gabe. It will be all right.

Elvis is stupid as hell.

I don't think we can count that as a track for my B side. Maybe a few seconds' worth of sound. Maybe I'll be able to fill the groove in later.

I'm so dumb for thinking this could work. Nobody was going to listen to my funky little show at midnight, especially on a community radio station that caters to middle-age people. Right? Then someone did, then more than one someone, but it was okay, because I was still just a voice in the dark. But now, between McSwingy's and this complete wreck of a date, Gabe's so far out in the light he's glowing. Right in the same town with all the people who think he's Liz.

I make it home, but I don't go inside—I pull a lawn chair up to the fountain and dangle my feet in it. It doesn't really help, but it grounds me a little. My heart slows down. The sun's fading out of the sky.

"How many times have I asked you not to put your feet in the fountain?" Mom. She comes up behind me and puts her hands on my shoulders. She hasn't touched me since I told her I was Gabe.

"About a million."

"So why do you still do it?" She's smiling. I can hear it in her voice.

"Because you told me not to. And it feels good on my feet."

She pats me, gently, like I might break. "Just do it when I'm not home, so I don't see you, all right?"

"Gotcha."

The grass rustles, and she's gone. I hear the door close. She might not hate me.

I pick up five pieces of landscape rock to wish on. Splash—someday I have a successful date with someone who's never met Liz. Splash—my mom looks at me again. Splash—I find a 45 of "Hot Pants." Splash—my dad looks at me again. Splash—Paige and I spend the rest of our lives together.

That's a lot of wishes for one fountain to hold, but nothing explodes. The water just bubbles along.

MORRISSEY SHOULD HAVE BEEN THE NEW ELVIS BUT HE COULDN'T GET PERMISSION FROM ELVIS'S ESTATE

Thursday evening at work. I keep thinking about Mara. If all dates are that stressful, I'm gonna be alone for the rest of my life—on purpose. Maybe she'll call. She might not. And if she does ask me out again, I might not go. And that's bullshit: of course I'll go. It's a girl, and she asked me out.

Chris wants me to dust, so I do, and I switch to thinking about songs for the Vibe contest. You wouldn't think there'd be songs about radio stuff, but there are tons, some of which are good and some of which are crazy boring.

Dusting is also good cover for watching girls. Not that I stare, but I watch. Heather Graves hasn't come by yet. I don't know if that's good or bad.

Lately I've been noticing how girls look alike, sort of like a herd. Lots of them have long straight hair, and they all wear layered tank tops with matching flip-flops. Their shorts are pretty short, and everyone carries an enormous purse. Sometimes Paige fits into the look-alike herd, but she usually chooses one accessory that helps her stand out, like tank tops in contrasting colors or cat-eye sunglasses, when everyone else has on the ones that completely cover their faces. She's smart like that.

After I dust one side of the store, I straighten up things behind the counter and add Paddy O'Furniture to the list of THE BEST BAND NAMES IN THE WORLD. Then a herd girl comes up to the counter, carrying a copy of Taylor Swift's latest. Eeew.

"Is there anything else I can help you with?" I have to ask because Chris says I have to ask, but I'd also love to help her turn those musical tastes into caviar instead of cat food.

"No thanks!" She's perky. Maybe it's a requirement to belong to the herd, but she has a cute smile, so that's something. Maybe her name is Ashley. She looks like an Ashley. Or an Amber. Something light and fluffy.

While I'm getting her CD into a bag, she does a double take at my nametag. "You're Gabe?"

"Uh … yeah."

"Like Gabe on the radio?"

Warning bells, sweaty hands, brain freakout. "Um … "

She's excited and talking fast. "Beautiful Music for Ugly Children? The Ugly Children Brigade?"

The part of my brain that's ready to go out with Mara

again is shouting OF COURSE IT'S ME! WHO ELSE WOULD IT BE? But the part that's afraid is trying to cover the first part's mouth.

"I…"

"His show is awesome! Midnight on Fridays, KZUK, if you're interested. We listen at the B side wall—we decorated it after the first show."

That must make her Becca, Sarah, or Maggie. Not like I've memorized who's on the B side wall or anything.

"One week we set up garden gnomes at Food Pride so they looked like they were shopping. We're on Facebook, too." She picks up her CD. "Hope to see you." She gives me a perky little wave as she moves out the door. The bell jingles when the door hits it, and the rings are just as perky as she is.

"You've gotta be kidding me." Chris is watching from the other side of the store.

"What?"

"She says 'Ugly Children Brigade' and you don't bust your ass to say 'yeah, that's me'?" Chris and I have gotten to be friends. "What the hell is wrong with you?"

"She was talking too fast. I couldn't get a word in."

"Yeah, right." Chris looks both amused and annoyed.

"It's one thing to be Gabe when nobody can see you. It's totally different to be out in broad daylight."

"So Gabe's really a vampire?"

"Look here, Mr. Minnesota Bland, you don't know anything about it." I could be pissed at him, but I'm not. I unpin my nametag from my shirt and throw it to him. "Since Gabe only comes out at night, I need a new name."

I'm brave, I'm chickenshit. I need to pick one.

He catches it with an odd look on his face. "Like what?" He pauses. "You know, a trans vampire could probably make a lot of bank in films."

"Being a trans vampire could be better than being a trans music geek. I'll look into it." I pick up the feather duster and start on the other side of the store.

By the time I'm done dusting, Chris has come back to the front counter and laid out seven different nametags on the glass counter. They say *MYRTLE, BETTY, HORATIO, CHET, ANGELA, YAO MING*, and *MR. SNUFFLEUPAGUS*, which almost doesn't fit in the space on the nametag. "Take your pick."

I pick up *BETTY* and pin it on. "I'll save *MR. SNUFFLEUPAGUS* for Mondays."

He gathers up the rest of them and puts them in the drawer. "I want to be *BETTY*, too, so don't hog it." He's saved out *CHET* and he puts it on.

"As long as I get to be *CHET* sometimes."

"No problem, *BETTY*."

"You should be *ANGELA* today. Your hair is very *ANGELA*-ish."

Chris flips his *ANGELA* mane at me and goes into the back room while I get to work making a table display of the remastered Beatles CDs. They're the starting point for all music and culture after 1962, according to John. Who am I to disagree? But there's still no point to "I Am the Walrus."

My phone vibrates. When I look, it says,

How r u today, sexy?

Excuse me?

I check the number, but there's no name. Someone will be pissed they didn't get it, and someone else will be pissed they didn't dial right.

I don't erase it. I can pretend it's from Paige.

After work I get gas and a Pepsi at the Kum & Go, also known as Ejaculate and Evacuate, because I need to drive around and listen to the Vibe. My brain chants it: *July 12, July 12, July 12.*

I'm on the way out the door when I almost run into a girl. We're both going too fast and not paying attention.

"'Scuse me." I duck and keep going, not looking at her.

"Gabe?"

Oh god. Not this soon.

"Mara, hey! How are you?" Immediately my mind goes to my looks, but I've been at McSwingy's, so I'm passing. Or passable, anyway.

"You left awfully fast yesterday."

"Sorry about that. Stuff to do, all that…"

"Let me get a coffee. Meet you back outside?" Big smile from Mara.

"Uh…sure."

Holy shit. Holy shit. Okay. Be cool.

Once she's paid for her gas and her coffee, Mara's at my car. "How are you?" She sips her froth and licks the foam off her lips. Sexy. I'm cheating again.

"I'm good. What's new since yesterday?" I give her a weak smile and take a swig of my Pepsi.

"I started teaching swimming lessons today." She fiddles with her coffee cup. "Five second-graders. Very loud. What did you do today?"

"Just…" I can't think. "…Worked."

"Where do you work?" Mara seems honestly interested.

"McSwingy's. Need to pad my music collection, you know." I hope she keeps going with the easy questions.

"Is that where you get all the stuff you play on your show? It must cost a lot to buy it all."

"Yeah, but my neighbor lets me mooch. His music library is so big I'll be thirty-five before I get through it all."

Mara smiles. "How come you never started a band?"

"I don't play an instrument. I took piano lessons for a while, but that's it."

"You're not even a band geek? Like 'this one time at band camp' band geek?" She's surprised.

"Nope."

"Me neither. But I always wanted to play something." She sighs. "It's a little late to start when you're a junior. Well, senior now."

The light is dim, but I can see she has on bright pink lip stuff. Her mouth looks like a strawberry. What a cliché. But it does.

"It's never too late to start something new." I take another swig of my Pepsi. "How often do you teach swimming lessons?"

"Every other…" Then she's staring at me. Like staring.

"What?"

"Pepsi."

No no no. I didn't even think of that. But it's too late. I can see it in her eyes.

"The snack bar. You'd always get a Pepsi from the machine." The puzzle pieces have clicked into place. "I told myself it wasn't you!" Now she's crying.

"Look, Mara ... "

"You're just ... messed up." She's backing away from me.

"Please just listen."

"Don't ever try to find me or talk to me again. You need help." In the dusk, the tears are heading towards her strawberry mouth.

"Please don't go." I reach for her hand.

She jerks back like I scalded her. "I liked you. I really did." One sob out loud, then she runs to her car. I can't look up when she screeches away.

Nobody here knows either of us. There was no shouting involved, and nobody made a scene. Just a conversation between two people.

Then it occurs to me: Mara will out me to the Ugly Children Brigade.

There's a garbage can close to my car, and I heave up all the Pepsi I drank, which wasn't much, but it feels like I'm throwing up from my toes. A couple walks by on the way to their car and I hear the woman say, "Gross! I bet that guy's drunk."

At least she said "guy."

When I'm done throwing up, I get in my car and drive

around for an hour, like I told myself I would. But I can't hear the Vibe for all the buzz in my head: *Out. Liz. Out. Gabe. Out. Mara. Out.*

Maybe it's good. Gabe 24/7. No more trans vampire act.

Yeah, right. It will not end well.

I have to pull over and puke again. But there's nothing there, so now my muscles hurt from the dry heaves.

I completely suck for thinking I could do this.

When I get home, I rush to my room. I dust my 45 to calm myself, then check the Ugly Children Brigade fan page. Nothing yet. Give her time.

What does Elvis have to say about the situation? *Don't be cruel. Stop, look, and listen. It's now or never.* He's full of clichés tonight.

Then I notice there's a box on my bed with a mailing label on it from Mango Products—the perfect ironic twist to the evening. I shove the box under my bed, with enough force to send it deep. I'm too freaked to open it right now.

It's obvious the powers of the universe are conspiring against me.

Or forcing my hand.

SCREEEEEEEEEECH. My new B side grooves are unwinding.

About three a.m., I check again. Mara's posted on the UCB page:

> Guess what? Gabe's not really … well, let's just
> say he's not who he says he is. I'm dropping out.
> He lied.

Then there are comments underneath the wall post: Who is he? and Why would he lie? and That can't be right. Then another Mara comment:

> Let's just say he's got the wrong equipment
> to be Gabe. That's all you need to know.

After that, somebody's written:

> You mean he doesn't have a turntable?

It could be a lot worse. A lot worse.

But I still can't sleep.

Friday night. I do the one-hit wonder show—without John, who's charming a lady friend. The CD he made me ages ago is full of great stuff—"Kung Fu Fighting" and "I'm Too Sexy" and "Crank Dat Soulja Boy" and, of course, "Come On Eileen"—but I suck because my mind is full of white noise. I remember to tell them about decorating someone's car, but I have no idea if they'll do it.

Maybe things will blow over. Mara will block the page and nobody will remember after a few weeks.

Then the show's over, and Marijane is gardening in her dirt. When I come out of the building, there are two guys standing in the parking lot. They've got on dark clothes and masks—Jason from *Friday the 13th* on one dude, and the mask from *Scream* on the other.

Guess there's always a first time to get pounded into the ground.

"Can I ... help you?" I don't know what else to say.

Jason, the tall one, throws a cig on the ground and grinds it out. "You Gabe?"

"Who's asking?"

"Me. You Gabe? We just need to know."

"Yeah."

Jason starts to laugh. "You're pathetic, you know that? We used to like your show." Scream doesn't say anything. They get in their car and peel out. I start to breathe again.

Whatever, fuckers. And masks? Maybe Mara sent them to scare me.

I do not need this right now.

CHUCK D. IS THE NEW ELVIS EVEN THOUGH HE SAYS EMINEM IS THE NEW ELVIS

Saturday. There are two pictures of decorated cars on the UCB page, so my brain has mostly quit fuzzing out. One car got painted—with washable car paint, just so you know, Gabe—like a clown, and one car got completely covered in helium balloons—they're tied to everything. The balloons all say *Get Well Soon!* and *Happy Retirement!* It was parked in front of the cop shop, which may have been the best part. But only two pictures, and that worries me. Usually there are more.

I check the friend number on the fan page, and it hasn't gone down—68, which is the highest it's ever been. So that's good.

If the UCB gives up on me because of Mara, I will not know how to act. My entire heart turns black when I think about it. I love them. And I made a scrapbook. A stupid goddamn scrapbook. Losing them scares me more than the dudes with the masks.

I get another text.

Hey sexy.

No name, just the number.

Maybe it's Paige, and she's using her dad's phone or something. She'd do that just to mess with me.

Everybody go away. I need peace.

I head to the back yard and stick my feet in the fountain, since my mom's gone. Then Paige wanders around the corner—with no call or text to warn me—and waves like she's the queen. I don't wave back, but she pulls up a lawn chair. "Gabey baby, what's new? I've got gossip for you."

Of course she does. "Did you text me a while ago with your dad's phone and say 'hey sexy'?"

"Why would I do that?"

"Just checking."

"You're dumb. And I wouldn't say you're sexy, really. More like cute." She flops her hand at me. "Maybe you have a secret admirer." She makes kissy faces.

"Whatever. Your gossip?"

She settles into her lawn chair, looking thoughtful. "You look crabby today."

"Long story." I'm not ready to talk yet.

"I canned Bobby X."

This surprises me. "I thought he was your truuuuu luuuuv."

"Knock it off. I need someone more fun, and he was a perpetual rain cloud."

"He was definitely bleak, and that scraggly goatee did nothing for him."

Now she doesn't look at me. "Guess you're my only boyfriend."

I don't look at her, either. "Guess so."

What the hell does that mean?

Then the cheerful Paige comes back. "So, why so crabby?"

This is gonna get weird. "Have you looked at the UCB page lately?"

"No."

"Um ... I met a girl." I whisper, just in case.

"Oh. You did?" She might be okay with it, or she might be pissed. Her face is neutral, but I'm betting on pissed.

"She's in the UCB," I say.

"I bet she called you at the station, didn't she? Like a fangirl." Still neutral, but with a dose of sarcasm. "Sure it's not her who texted you?"

"She doesn't have my number. But she goes to West."

"So? It's a big place."

"She knows I was Liz, so she outed me to the UCB."

Paige's eyes are wide. "How'd she figure it out?"

"Snack bar change."

"What?"

"She used to give me change at the snack bar."

She sits back, and I can see she's still working on the neutrality. "Well. Hmm. Now what?" A pause. "I thought I was the only girl in your life." I'm right about the pissed part. "And I thought BFFs told each other everything."

"You are, and you're right, but I didn't want to tell you because I didn't want you to give me shit." I'm not going to tell her about the mask guys because I don't want to hear about them, either. She'll tell me to go to the police, because she believes in law and order. I, on the other hand, believe the police won't care about someone like me.

Paige snorts. "Of course I'm going to give you shit. That's what friends are for." Then, of course, she has ideas. "You could just deny it. Or you could quit the show, go someplace where no one knows you, and start it up again. Or you could join the circus!" Her voice gets louder with each sentence.

I glare. "Keep it down." Then I realize I haven't told her that the Vibe said yes. "I have news related to moving away."

"You're joining the circus because you got outed?"

Another glare in her direction. "Do you remember when John entered me into the contest to compete for a radio show at the Vibe?"

"Nope."

"For someone who claims to be my BFF and wants to know everything, you sure don't remember much."

She rolls her eyes. "How about when we were fifteen

133

and you decided you wanted to be a lumberjack? Move up north to Ely and learn how to hack down trees? That was hilarious."

"Okay, well, anyway, I'm a finalist in the contest, and I still get to do it as Gabe."

"But you entered as Elizabeth?"

"John didn't know, then."

"Have you guys started planning what you're going to do?"

"I've started, but it's ... " Then I remember what I found on my bed the other day and I jump up like a snake bit me on the ass. "I forgot the Mango!"

Paige stares. "You have major issues today."

"It's here."

"Are you wearing it?"

"Look at me."

She checks out my baggy shorts. "So where is it?"

"Hidden."

We go inside to scope the scene. My mom is home now, and unloading groceries. She hears us and comes out of the kitchen. "Hi, ladies. Want a Popsicle?"

I try to shove Paige up the stairs. "No thanks."

"I'd love a Popsicle!" She's sweet to parents. Nobody knows her evil side but me.

I give Paige a dark look as she heads into the kitchen to get herself a Popsicle. She smirks over her shoulder. "Sure you don't want one, Gabe?"

I see my mom twitch just a little when she hears Paige say that name, but she goes back to the groceries. "Later, girls."

"Bye!" Paige is cheery to the point of nausea.

There's no lock on my bedroom door, so I stack three boxes of albums in front of it, to warn us if someone barges in, and then I try to find the Mango. I have to crawl under my bed, on my stomach, past boxes of eight-tracks to get it out.

Paige is perched on my desk chair, laughing. "You were afraid someone would open your package?"

"Funny pun." My voice is muffled because I'm still under my bed.

"In my house, mail is private."

I find a dusty box of CDs. "You just don't know."

"It's not like the box is the shape of a penis!"

"So?" I find a dress my mom tried to make me wear when I was confirmed in seventh grade. That fight was enormous. "And don't use that word."

"Box?"

"Shut up."

She laughs and takes it from me when I emerge from the wilderness. "When did it get here?"

"Thursday."

She starts tugging at the packing tape. "And you didn't open it yet? What the hell is wrong with you?"

"Getting outed took up my brain power, plus I had to do a show."

"You have dust bunnies in your hair." Paige smirks.

"I do?"

"Let me . . ." She slides them out, but gives my hair a

yank as well, what she can grab of it. "Open it already, Mr. Security."

"Hand me those scissors." I point at a pair on my desk, and she does, then I slice open the tape and pull it out. It's soft and pinkish, and it looks like a dick. Mostly.

"What's this for?" Paige points to the funnel thingy.

"You push it against your, you know … where you pee … and it comes out the end of the … prosthetic."

Paige doesn't seem bothered at all. "Got it. Gonna try it on?"

She can't be serious. "Right here? In front of you?"

"You show me yours, I'll show you mine. Remember when we did that? We were what—six?"

"But it's a dick!"

"So what? I've seen a dick before. Need some help?"

"Can it. And turn around." I fish out the directions.

Paige points to the harness and straps. "What's that for?"

"When you wear it with boxers, you need this. Tighty whiteys hold it on so you don't need the strap."

She stretches out on top of the comforter my mom picked out when I was fifteen. Ugly and girly. "Are you gonna try it on or not?"

"Dammit, I said TURN AROUND."

"I'm turned around." She rolls over and puts her back to me, so I shuck off my shorts.

"Shall I take off my clothes, too?" I hear the mischief in her voice.

"One almost-naked teenager is enough." She doesn't know what my boy brain would do with that information.

It takes me a minute to figure out how to hook it up, and she taps her fingers on the wall. "Haven't you ever worked a penis before? I can give you some tips."

My whole body is hot and flushed, and I've never felt more naked in my life, but I think I've got it right. "You can turn back around."

She does, and her eyes go straight to my crotch. The Mango hangs where it should. My skin doesn't match its color, but it's close enough for accidental glances at the urinal. The harness feels odd, but nobody should see it under the boxers. I'll get used to it.

It's all I can do not to cover myself with my hands.

Paige studies me. "Hmm. Okay then."

"That's all you can say?"

"What do you want me to say? 'Gee, Gabe, nice dick'?"

"I don't know!"

She can see how freaked I am. "This has to feel a little surreal."

"You think?"

"Are you sure you don't want me to show you mine?" She unsnaps her pants.

"I already have one of those, and I really, really wish you'd shut up about yours." She has no idea how much I wish she'd shut up.

"Let's find a teen night in the Cities and try it out. You can pee at the urinals this time."

Paige turns around again, and I slip out of the Mango harness and tuck everything into my boy undies drawer. All of a sudden, relief pours over my head, shoulders, heart, like someone is drowning me with goodness. I don't know if I believe in God, but there must be Somebody up there if there's something like a Mango. I try to be quiet as I'm shuffling the boxers, but Paige hears me sniffle.

"Gabe?" Her hand is on my back.

I turn to her, and she can see I'm trying not to cry. But my nose is beginning to run.

"I'm glad for you."

"Yeah." And then I can't help it. Paige holds me and pats me on the back as the tears gush, and I let myself be held. Finally I'm back to a runny nose.

Paige pats me one more time. "That was a girly thing to do." She reaches out and smoothes my eyebrows. "Not like these caterpillars. Why don't you pluck?"

I break away from her and punch her in the arm. "Don't tell anybody you saw me do that." I shut the drawer.

"Who am I gonna tell?" Paige's summer-blue eyes are wide and bright when I look at her. And kind. "Better now?"

I smile at her. "Sometimes you're really nice."

"What do you mean, sometimes?" She flops on my bed again. "We should see what Mara's saying on Facebook."

"No thanks."

"Oh, come on." Paige is still lying there, looking for all the world like one of those women in a really old painting, *la la la and where is the house boy with my grapes*, that kind of thing. "It'll be fine. I think you're pretty damn convincing as a man, especially lately."

"What if I was wearing a nametag that said *BETTY*?"

"Why the hell would you do that?"

I laugh. "I'm *MR. SNUFFLEUPAGUS* on Mondays."

"You guys are off the chain." She rolls her eyes. Paige thinks Chris is a loser druggie, which he used to be, but so what?

Paige hops off the bed and picks up my iPod—my graduation present to myself, engraved with *GABE 24/7* on the back. "Have you got 'Flashdance' on here?" She starts thumbing through and comes up with it on a playlist called *'80s crap* that I made for her. "The eighties are not crap, and watch this. I memorized her moves so I can use them when we club." She puts the iPod in its dock on my desk and points to the bed. "Go sit."

I do. Even though she looks like a cross between a butterfly and a spazzed-out sparrow, it works. Then the song's done and she's out of breath, looking at me like she doesn't know whether I'm going to holler at her or laugh. "So?"

I don't know what to say, because she looks more beautiful at this moment than she's ever looked. "Wow."

She's annoyed. "That's all you can say—'wow'? I wasn't better than 'wow'?"

"No! You were … fantastic. Amazing. Breathtaking. Gorgeous." I stop, because I'm getting close to the truth.

"That's better." Now she looks pleased, and she flounces over to the bed and sits next to me. "Maybe I can do it some night at Happiness."

I scoot away from her. "Maybe some night when I'm not there, so you don't embarrass me."

She scoots next to me again, then pushes my shoulder down so I'm lying on my back with my legs dangling off the bed. Once I'm down, she snuggles up next to me. "We make good dance partners, don't you think?"

My BFF has just curled up to me like I'm a guy. Her guy.

I sit up in a hurry. "What the hell are you doing?" She can't just switch like that. I need some warning.

She sits up, too, with wide eyes that are trying to look innocent, but she can't quite pull it off. "What?"

I get off the bed, casual as can be, and grab for my iPod in its dock. Nothing like changing the subject. "You've gotta hear the play list John made me." It's mostly Public Enemy, with a little Nas and OutKast, plus a dollop of Lil Wayne. I start it up and add a head bob, hoping she'll follow my lead.

"Okay." I see the question in her eyes, but then she takes off again, shaking her ass and rippling her stomach like Beyoncé. It's honestly not much better than lying on the bed next to her, because she's sexy as the day is long.

Then we stomp—literally—about a hundred times around the room to "Bring tha Noize." Public Enemy and Anthrax, as unlikely a pair as me and Paige. But there it is, on a playlist. And here we are. At some point, I look at her face, and I would almost swear the invisible word on her forehead is *POSSIBLE*.

My mom hollers up the stairs, so loud we hear her through the door. "What in God's name are you doing? You're shaking the light fixtures!"

We open the door and yell back. "Sorry!"

"And turn it down! I can hear that stuff all the way down here."

"We'll quit. Sorry!" Paige is way more charming than I am. "Thanks, girls" is the response, so Paige has done her job.

When Paige goes home, after supper and after my folks make us play Monopoly with them and Pete, I collapse. After the bed incident I made sure there was no chance for us to be alone, which is stupid, because why wouldn't I want her to curl up to me? But it scared me. What if it went wrong?

I can't even contemplate it.

I click into Facebook. Liz and her one friend. Pathetic. Then, when I look at the fan page for the Ugly Children Brigade, there's a new post, by a guy named Jason SerialKiller, with a Jason mask as his profile picture.

> It's not just a turntable issue—YOU NEED TO KNOW GABE IS REALLY LIZ WILLIAMS—not a guy. Thank you Mara for the clue. Liz is the IT who went to West. She lied. Now we're going to fuck IT up. Nobody that sick should be allowed to live.

I call Paige.
"I just left!"
"Look at the UCB page."
Silence while she turns on her computer.
"Do you see it?" I try to keep the shake out of my voice.
"Who is this asshole?"

"He was in the parking lot at the station Friday, when I came out."

Instant anger. "Why didn't you tell me? Did he hurt you?"

"He just asked if I was Gabe. How was I supposed to know he wanted to kill me?"

"We've got to go to the police." Now she's got her *don't mess with me* voice on.

"No."

"You are so fucking dense. This isn't funny!"

"The cops won't care."

"Don't be dumb! What if you get hurt?"

"I'll figure it out."

"Dammit, Gabe!" Now she's almost crying.

"Look." I take a deep breath and scan the Facebook page again. "If there's more, we'll go to the cops. Next time he posts, him or his friend." I'm brave. Brave, brave, brave. And I'm shaking so hard I can barely hold my phone.

"There was more than one?"

"A guy in a Scream mask."

"I'm coming over right now."

"No!" But she's hung up.

I meet her in the driveway before she's had time to storm my house. She's pissed. "You get in this car right now and let's go."

"If something else happens, then yes. Right now, he's just talking shit." In the time it took her to get here, I've calmed down and thought it over. That's all it is. Just talking shit.

"You are so fucking stubborn!" There's a tear on her cheek, and she wipes it away.

"Be happy about that, or I would've given up on you a long time ago." I manage a grin, so she knows I'm not serious, but she hits me anyway.

"For that, I'm leaving."

"Good." Another smile.

She backs out fast and burns away, but I know she's not really mad. If she was mad, she would have erased my number from her phone. I've seen her do that before.

One more time, she's got my back. I love her for that.

When I go back inside, my mom hollers at me. "Was that Paige again?"

"She just came back to get her iPod."

"All right." And that's that.

Suddenly I want to go to her and say, "Guess what, Mom? I got asked out by a girl, then she outed me, then I got threatened, and now I just want to quit. Okay? Can I quit? I don't want to be Gabe anymore." I want to hug her and put my head on her lap and cry. I want her to stroke my hair and say, "Shhhh, honey, it's all right. It will be all right." Because maybe then it would be.

I watch the Facebook page. Six people write variations of the same question: Are you sure? Each time, Jason says Yup. Once a person named Scream GonnaGetCha says, We are definitely sure. His profile picture is a Scream mask.

At three a.m. there are 57 members, down from 68. By five a.m., it's 54.

I go to bed. When I wake up at noon, it's 42. I scan the friend list. Heather is still there, but Mara is gone.

I can't think what else to do, so I write it in the scrapbook—*R.I.P. Ugly Children Brigade*—on the page after the decorated cars. I take a screen shot of the page and print it off, so I can remember. I don't know what happens when a page hits zero. Does Facebook take it down?

If it's in a scrapbook, I can say it happened. It was real once.

SIMON COWELL IS THE NEW ELVIS BECAUSE SIMON SAID SO; JUST TRY AND ARGUE WITH HIM

One a.m. Wednesday morning, in my room. I've spent four hours listening to the Vibe after work, wondering how I'm going to do that show. I've got a vision: five hundred people milling around, me on stage smiling and grooving along, playing every good song about radio. A serious outdoor dance party. Then Jason and Scream come tearing through the crowd and shoot me.

They're just douchebags, blowing off their mouths. Right? And there are still 39 UCB friends, so it's not dead yet.

Elvis, what do I do now?

Viva Las Vegas.

Wrong answer.

It's all right, Gabe. They're just dicks.

You sure about that?

Silence.

My bedroom window is open, and John is having a hoedown with Trace Adkins, of all people. I slip downstairs and sneak outside, quiet as can be, and knock on his door.

He's not surprised to see me, and he steps back to let me in. "Shouldn't you be in bed?"

"I came over to find out why the hell you like Trace Adkins."

"Trace Adkins, Joe Nichols, Blake Shelton, country stars are interchangeable these days." He goes to turn down the stereo. "In my day, there were people worth listening to. George Jones. Merle Haggard. Even Hank Williams—not Junior, but the first one." He seems personally offended by the whole situation. "This bland crap sounds like wallpaper paste."

"I didn't know wallpaper paste had a sound."

"You know what I mean, smartass."

"So why are you even listening?"

"I have no idea." He switches Trace Adkins out for some Johnny Cash. "Much better. Forgive me for slipping in my musical judgment and exposing you to such bullshit. And what do you want, by the way?"

I slump on the couch. "Have you seen the UCB page lately?"

"No. Should I look?"

"Probably."

John goes into a music bedroom to get his laptop, and he pulls up the page. "Hmm. Lots going on." He reads some more, then puts the laptop away and comes back to sit down. "They're just haters."

"Yeah, but what if they mean it?"

"Then we'll go to the cops. The end."

Not them again. "The cops will not give a flying shit about me."

"You don't know that." John is calm. "Everyone deserves to be safe."

"I'm not betting on it." Macho cops plus trans person equals sketchy situation.

I think he knows changing the subject is the best idea. "For now, though, you need help with your Vibe show. Do you have a list?"

"Mostly."

"Let me hear it, then. How much time do you need to fill?"

"Half an hour, so with talking in between, I figure I need five songs around four minutes long, plus my secret song: 'WOLD,' Chapin. 'Nightfly,' Fagen. 'Mexican Radio,' Wall of Voodoo. 'Radio,' Rancid. 'Radio Free Europe,' REM. 'Radio Gaga,' Queen. I want to be pretty broad."

"Maybe you should check out some country."

"I know." I start picking at the frayed seams on his couch. I need to fidget. Then I try to pick a hole in the couch cushion. "That's another thing."

"What's another thing?"

"Girls."

John laughs. "Topic switch. What makes you think I know anything about girls?"

"You know more than me." The couch is now resisting my efforts. "It's Paige."

"Your too-smart friend? What about the other girl who asked you out? Called you at the station?"

"She's the one who outed me to the Ugly Children Brigade because she knew Liz from school."

He chuckles. "Of course you don't have a turntable. You always come over here and borrow mine."

"Only a dinosaur like you would have one."

"Hey now, people are putting out vinyl again."

"Like who?"

"Avenged Sevenfold. Tegan and Sara. And Warner Brothers just released a bunch of old stuff—Clapton, Fleetwood Mac, Tom Petty. Back to the original topic. Maybe people don't care about your lack of a turntable."

"Since my new friends Jason and Scream posted, the UCB has lost 29 people."

"Well ... " John shrugs. "It's their problem, not yours."

"Easy for you to say, because you don't know." It is so fucking easy for everyone else to talk about this like it's not a big deal.

"No, I don't. But it's true—it's not you. It's them." He can see me gritting my teeth. "You don't believe me, do you?"

"Not right now."

"Well, maybe someday."

"Someday's not soon enough."

"It's all you've got, son. And someday might be tomorrow." The look on his face tells me he's been down the someday road before. "It'll get better. Now tell me something happy."

So I go get the laptop again and show him the *OH SHIT* photos, which are now the only evidence it happened because we had a huge rain that washed all the chalk off both schools. He laughs so hard he chokes.

Then he settles down in his chair while I put the laptop away again. "So anyway, back to your smart friend."

I go back to the couch. "She keeps giving me … signals. And I don't know what they mean."

"Give me examples."

"Well, she likes to club with me, and she tells me I'm her boyfriend. And a few days ago she snuggled up to me in my bedroom." Just thinking about it gives me shivers, from fear or pleasure I don't know.

"Maybe she likes Gabe more than she thinks she does."

"But we've been friends since kindergarten!" Now I'm sure the shivers are from panic. "I can't wreck it now! I mean … yeah, I'd love it, but … " I bury my face in my hands.

"You like her, all right. You might even love her." He's grinning.

"You don't know that." My face stays in my hands, so he can't see me blush.

"Yes I do. Otherwise you wouldn't be like this. Does she know you like her as a girlfriend?"

"Hell no! And I don't have what she wants."

John gets up to grab some Pepsi for each of us. "If you haven't asked, you can't know what she wants."

"Come on."

"What does it mean to 'have what she wants'?" He brings me a glass, and I swig it down.

"You know … having … well, not having a coochie snorcher." I can't tell him about the Mango. This is hard enough.

John sips his Pepsi. "Being a man isn't just about your dick."

"That's because you actually have a dick. You don't have to think about it." I pause. "At least I assume you have a dick."

We have just opened another new door in this relationship.

"I have a dick, yes." John sips again. "Thank god for Viagra. But being a man is just being a person who happens to have a penis." He gets up to refill my empty Pepsi glass. "If being a guy includes flirting with Paige, then flirt with her, and let her flirt with you. Or not. Your choice."

When John comes back from the kitchen, he hands me my glass, then waves me back into the music room. "Can we work on your radio show?"

I check my watch. "Dude, it's one thirty." When we get going, we can goof around until the sun comes up. "I have to work tomorrow."

"What time?"

"Noon."

He gives me his best *oh come on, you know you want to look.* "I'll be good, I promise." He's the one who gets us in trouble, because he's always showing me new stuff and new bands. "We can look for a secret song."

So we turn on the Vibe for a while to analyze what it's playing, even though it's the middle of the night and a night show isn't like an evening show—different audiences and all that. Then we go back to the music rooms and start to dig. The next time I look at the clock, it's 4:30 a.m.

It's actually not John's fault that we can mess with his stuff for so long. When I'm mixing playlists, I have fantasies. Maybe the guest spot at the Vibe will turn into a job, and I'll become the biggest jock in the history of the station. Maybe I'll get hormones by Christmas. Maybe I'll get to officially change my name by February. Maybe Paige and I can get married once I'm legally a guy. Maybe, maybe, maybe. Sometimes I make lists of wedding dance music, music to celebrate hormones by, music to recover from surgery with. I will use them someday. I've promised myself.

Maybe there will be a day when this shit will be over and I can just be a dude with normal, regular stuff in his life. If you think about it, I'm already there. I have a job, worry about girls, and listen to loud music in my car like other guys. It's everybody else who doesn't see it that way.

When the headphones are tight on my ears, the sounds slide into my bloodstream like little silver fish, racing and flashing. Music doesn't hurt me. It's love that just loves you, and doesn't care who you are or what's between your legs.

Music is safe.

When I get home, I dust my 45 again, then I check the UCB page to see the fan number—which is 31. There's a new post from Jason SerialKiller:

> We're coming to get you, IT. Be ready. You'll never
>   know when, you'll never know how, but we're
>   watching. Dead. Bam. Over.

My hands are shaking so badly I can barely click the page closed. So much for safety.

I go brush my teeth and try not to let my toothbrush vibrate out of my mouth. When I get back to my room, there's a text from the mystery number:

> Why no txt back? Grad party? Saw fb posts.
>   No turntable is okay. U r sexy. :)

Holy mother of wow.

Paige can never touch my phone again. Some kind of radar

will go off and she'll read my texts, and then she'll run over my phone with her car. But I can't erase it. It's too good.

Is this what being a grown-up is like? Badness and goodness squished together in a big ball of craziness?

I sit very still and stare out my window until the sun comes up.

AMY WINEHOUSE IS THE NEW ELVIS BECAUSE DRUGS WEREN'T NICE TO HER CAREER, EITHER

Friday morning, maybe eight thirty. My phone vibrates next to my head.

R u there, sexy?

I laugh. Give me an hour, my chest binder, and my Mango. Then we can talk about sexy. I text back.

I'm here.

I have to take it back. I can't talk to her. But the electrons are gone, speeding through the air. Then I'm more excited than a kid at Christmas. A beautiful, luscious, gorgeous girl thinks I'm sexy. Then I'm petrified. Then I want to laugh. Then have a heart attack.

Of course I can't go back to sleep. When I go downstairs, the paper is spread all over the dining room table like it is every morning, but my dad's still there, eating eggs. Pete's there too, eating a bowl of cereal, the milk and a box of Peanut Butter Captain Crunch in front of him. Mom's drinking a cup of coffee and scanning the front page.

I go find a bowl and bring it back to the table. My dad glances up. "How are you today ... Elizabeth?"

"I'm Gabe. How are you?"

"Just fine." He finishes his eggs and leaves, giving my mom a kiss on the way. The door bangs as he goes into the garage.

"Pete, what's new?" I pour milk on my cereal and pull a section of the paper toward me.

"Nothin'." That's a long sentence for him in the morning. His cereal is gone, so he picks up his bowl and heads into the kitchen, taking Dad's plate with him. The dishwasher opens and closes, and then I hear him going back upstairs.

"Is he going to work?"

"He's going to bed. He's back in the baby phase." My mom doesn't look up.

"What?"

"Eat, sleep, poop, and repeat. That's about all he's good for right now, except for trips to Target."

"I had no idea."

"I think it's just teenage boys that go through it. You never did."

I could take it personally that she reminded me I'm not a teenage boy, but I play it cool. "Maybe it'll happen later. You never know."

She realizes what she's said. "Well, um ... maybe in college. That's a good place to sleep all the time—once you've gone to class, that is."

I hear the oven ding, and Mom gathers up the paper. "Cookies are done." She heads into the kitchen.

"Can I have one?" I follow her in with my empty cereal bowl. The radio's tuned to one of the less-talk-more-music stations from the Cities, something that's supposed to be for women. Boring

She spreads the paper on the counter. "Get away. No. They're for work." She works at a daycare in the afternoons. She gets the cookie sheet close to the counter, sliding the cookies onto the newspaper.

I grab one of the warm ones and shove it in my mouth. "Mrgfswrw."

"Elizabeth, that wasn't nice."

I swallow the cookie. "My name's not Elizabeth."

"Legally, it is." She's lining cookies up in neat rows. "So I should still be able to call you Elizabeth."

It's too freaking early in the morning. "That may be true, but I'd prefer you call me Gabe." I keep my voice calm.

She's washing cookie sheets. "It's just ... hard. You have this sweet little baby, and then, all of a sudden, she tells you it's a mistake. We created a mistake." She's scrubbing a hole in the metal.

"What?" I have no idea what she means.

"Dad and I made you, and you said that being a girl was a mistake."

That's what I said when I told them about Gabe. "Not like that!"

She's dried off her hands and is rearranging the cookies with her spatula, shoving them around like hockey pucks on slick ice. "You don't talk to us. You don't eat with us. You don't answer your cell phone. You spend all your time with John and Paige, or working. Yesterday I needed you to go get milk, and you wouldn't call me back."

"I'm sorry. I'll work on it. And you wanted me to get a job!"

She retrieves the second cookie sheet from the oven and shuffles the cookies to the counter. When she turns to wash it, I see a tear on her cheek.

"Mom?" My mother doesn't cry.

"This is my fault!" Now she's sobbing, slumped against the counter, dishtowel pressed against her face.

I don't know what to do. "What could be your fault?"

I hear a little snort. She lowers the dishtowel. "Somehow our genes screwed you up, or something went wrong when I was carrying you, so this is my fault. Gabe is my fault."

I've probably hugged my parents less than five times in the last five years, but if there was ever a time to do it, it's right now. I go to her and put my arms around her. "It isn't anybody's fault. It just happens."

She hugs me hard and pulls away. "It's not anybody's fault *but* mine. You marinated in my body for nine months." The tears keep coming. "And you didn't tell us what was wrong until the end of your senior year! What kind of crappy parents are we that we pushed away our child?"

They've always stressed the "we're here for you" idea, so me not sharing is a huge deal. They have no idea I haven't been sharing since middle school. I always found something to tell them when they asked what was wrong, but it usually wasn't the actual thing.

"It was just . . . complicated. And I did try to tell you, when I was a kid. But you thought I was making things up."

She studies me, leaning against the counter with her red eyes. Her look is daggers now. "Do you trust me?"

I have to look away from that fierceness. "Yes. As much as I can."

She sweeps her arms wide and hits the dirty bowls and measuring cups from making cookies, which crash into the sink with a huge noise. "Nothing you could do would make me not love you. Nothing!"

I've never seen my mom like this.

"I know I've been a crappy mom for the last couple months." She takes both my hands and looks me square in the eye. "But no matter what, no matter how strange it is, you are still my precious baby. I'm your first defender and last champion. Forever. Even if I don't always call you by your new name." She bursts into tears again, so I hug her some more while she sobs, but she pulls it together pretty quickly. I don't think she wants me to see how sad she is.

When she finally looks up, she squeezes my face between her hands. "It'll be fine. We'll be sure it's fine." Her look is fierce, and I don't know if she can see what's happening to me, but all the tears she cried are threatening to fall out of my eyes, too. I don't deserve this kind of love.

Nobody says anything for a second. Then she kisses me, lets my face go, picks up a warm cookie, and hands it to me. "Go do something useful, all right?"

"You got it." I hug her again. Now I've hugged my mom three times in the last ten minutes, so I'm covered for the next two years. "Thank you." I whisper it into her ear.

"That's what parents are for."

I leave with my cookie before she decides to take it back. Any of it. All of it.

There's another text:

Want 2 meet up?

I text back:

For real? Or r u just flirting?

We'll see what she says.

If Paige got crabby when she learned about Mara, she would lose it over this. At least I hope she would.

When I look out the window, John is puttering around in his yard. By the time I make it over there he's pulled a bunch of weeds in a flowerbed.

"Hey, John."

He whirls around like I've smacked him. "Holy smokes,

Liz! Don't do that!" Then he corrects himself. "Gabe. I mean Gabe. Sorry." His face tells me he really is sorry.

"Want to help me plan a show for tonight? Or we could work on the Vibe show."

"Whichever." He wipes his hands on his shorts. "I'm not helping these flowers out anyway." He sets a sprinkler to rain on them and we go inside. After he washes his hands and gets us Pepsis, we go back to the music rooms.

"So what strikes your fancy?"

"I have no concept." And I don't. It's only ten a.m.

"Why not do an Elvis show tonight? Honor your rock and roll hero. The world would be a whole different place without him."

"That's what you always say about the Beatles."

"Them, too. But Elvis is different." He clears a space near his computer, then grabs a bunch of stuff from all the different rooms, including a shoebox. The stack must be three feet high. "This will get us started. Do you have to work today?"

"Nope, but we've got to be at the station in thirteen hours. That enough time?"

He grins. "It's not like we have to listen to it all. But why not?"

By hour two, we're hungry, which makes sense, since it's lunchtime, so John calls Domino's and they deliver while Elvis is singing "How Great Thou Art" at the top of his lungs. The guy gives John the fish eye when he gives John the pizza and says, "Gross." John says, "Better music than will ever come out of your pie hole, sonny," and the pizza guy goes away.

While we're eating, Paige calls, and I tell her about our Elvis festival and would she like to come with us to the station tonight? She's been bugging me again. She says yes, and hangs up after she reconfirms that we are the biggest dorks in Maxfield and she'd rather read right now, but pick her up at 11:30.

By the end of four hours, we've listened to six of the seventy-two RCA albums, all the Sun singles, and all thirty extended-play singles, and I'm a little sick of Elvis. It's useful to know you can overdose on a good thing. At some point, I started flicking my Zippo every time the song changed, and when the songs are two minutes long that's a lot of lighter fluid, so I'm almost out.

Finally I can't stand it any longer. "I think I've had enough of the King. How about you?"

John is blissed out on his couch, looking like a very happy dead man. "We haven't done any live albums."

"Can we switch to Elvis Costello, at least?"

"That might be acceptable. But just early stuff." He gets up, and Elvis is cut off in the middle of "Mystery Train." It wasn't helping that John was going from fifties Elvis to seventies Vegas Elvis then back again, which can make you seasick. Then "No Action" blasts from the speakers, Costello's first song on *This Year's Model*, one of the best albums in the history of British punk.

"Better?" He doesn't seem happy to have lost the real Elvis.

"Much." I start slam dancing even though there's really nothing to slam into, just for fun and because I know it annoys John.

"Cut it out. You'll skip the album." John is stern about skips. "Come in here. I want to show you something."

I gently slam into his shoulder as I hop through the door. "What is it?"

"Why should I tell you when I can show you? You may never tell another living soul. And stop that hopping stuff. Right now."

I stand still. "Yes, sir." He's serious.

John goes around to the counter by his laptop and picks up the shoebox he brought in four hours ago when we started getting our Elvis on. "I don't get it out much. Like once every ten years. Can't let anyone see it."

"Must be pretty rare."

"You have no idea." John's digging through the box, and he comes up with what looks like a napkin. He hands it to me. "Be gentle."

The napkin says, *To the best DJ in town, keep your show Red Hot and Blue. Your friend Elvis.*

I read the words again and again. "This isn't real. It can't be."

"The hell it's not. July 1954, Memphis, Tennessee, 'That's All Right,' flip side 'Blue Moon of Kentucky,' and when I interviewed him, I said, 'You, boy, are gonna be big. Sign this, will you, so I can say I knew you when,' and he did. And there it is."

I can't stop staring. "You could sell this for a thousand dollars. Maybe more."

"Why would I do that?" He takes it away from me. "When I die, you can sell it or frame it or whatever you want, but right now, it's the only piece of my youth I have."

A little flare goes off in my brain. "The 45 I have is the same one you played that night?" I knew it was an original pressing, but I didn't know it was that exact 45.

"You got it."

"That's worth way more than the autograph—ten thousand dollars, at least!"

"So sell it when you need some cash." John doesn't put the autograph back in the box. Instead he pulls out a piece of paper and unfolds it. "I'd forgotten this was in here."

It's a child's drawing of a house. Around the house it says, "I love you Dad." It's clear John doesn't want me to look at it, because he folds it back up pretty quickly.

"From your daughter?" I know he has at least one daughter, because he's got a picture of her in his kitchen, a tiny little girl in a pretty dress that looks like it's from the sixties.

"From my son." He won't look at me.

"You had a son, too?"

"I still have a son. Patrick. He's forty-five and lives in Seattle. My daughter Margaret is forty-eight and lives in Chicago. Their mother passed away about fifteen years ago."

This is almost as amazing as the Elvis napkin.

Elvis Costello is frenetic in the background, but he's so out of place I shut him off. "How old were your kids when your wife left you?"

"Thirteen and ten. About the age you were when I met you." He gives me a sad smile. "I got lucky when I got you as a neighbor. The fact that you liked music? Double bonus. But I think I turned your music hobby into a psychotic obsession."

"Psychotic obsessions give you something to do." I'm trying to make him laugh because he looks so sad. "So I was the kid you didn't have anymore?"

"More like a grandkid."

"What else is in that box?"

"Just memories." He pulls a bottle cap from the bottom of the box. "Like this."

I check it out. "A cap from a Guinness pint? That stuff looks like sand."

"Bitter and thick, just like me. But I've been off the stuff since June 26, 1979." He flips it into my hand. "Read the date."

Written inside the bottle cap is *6-26-74*. "They imported Guinness to the US in 1974?"

"That's not what matters. That's the day they left me."

"You wrote it down on a bottle cap?"

"It was the biggest day of my life. Then I proceeded to get wrecked out of my mind every single day for the next five years. What else are you supposed to do when you drive your family away?" His voice is so quiet I can barely hear him.

I have no idea what to say, to that statement or to any of it. "I'm sorry."

"Me too." He takes the bottle cap back from me, looking like someone's died.

"Maybe we should do something else." Once John's put the bottle cap in it, I put the lid back on the box and move it to a shelf across the room.

"I think that's wise." He swipes at his eyes. "When you walk down memory lane, you gotta watch out for the boulders. But as long as we're telling secrets, I've got one more." He opens the closet door, shoves stuff around, then pulls out a battered, crap-ass guitar.

"Okay." It's not impressive, as secrets go.

"This came from Tupelo, Mississippi."

Scratch that. This secret is huge. Giant. Elvis got a guitar from Tupelo Hardware when he was eleven, which has to mean the guitar in John's hand is one of the most revered pieces of American music history. Legend says Elvis wanted a rifle instead, but he took what his mom gave him.

"How the hell did you get it?"

"Won it off a guy in Vegas in a backroom poker game."

"How much is it worth?" I'm trying not to shit bricks. "The beginning of rock and roll is in your closet, dude!"

He smiles at me, though the sadness about his family is still in his face. "Someday it's yours."

"No way." I could never be trusted with something that amazing.

"Let's not worry about it now." He puts the guitar way, way in the back of the closet.

"Right, or I'll start worrying about robbers breaking in and killing you just for that guitar."

John comes back to the table. "Let's get to work, huh?"

"You didn't have to show that stuff to me."

"You told me your secret. I should tell you some of mine." He busies himself in the crates on the floor under the computer. "How about that Elvis show? And who shut off Costello?"

I switch him back on, though I'm still thinking about the guitar. "Lipstick Vogue" explodes into the room. "He didn't seem appropriate to the conversation."

"We should've had old country drinking songs on," John says. Now he's a little more like the John I know, not the one caught in the past. "Tonight, let's go chronological with Elvis, but let's do it all: gospel, Vegas, singles, everything."

"You got it." And for the next two hours we put together fifty minutes of Elvis's best. Somewhere in there I swear I hear a *thank you* in my head, but I'm not sure. Maybe Elvis is glad to get some airtime.

We're at the station and John's settled in the corner of the booth with a Pepsi and a cigarette, not lit, just one he's playing with. Paige is in the other corner trying not to touch stuff, but she'd mess with everything if I'd let her.

"Welcome, welcome, friends, to Beautiful Music for Ugly Children, and a special welcome to the UCB. I'm Gabe, of course, and tonight is an Elvis night. Why Elvis? He's only the man who blended bluegrass, country, and rhythm and blues all together, and he brought the world a whole new style. Not to mention a whole new set of jokes about his sad old fat self long after he changed the musical world. Poor man. To start us off, here's the one that got him going, first played in Memphis in 1954 by this town's own John Burrows."

John's waving, telling me to stop, but I keep going.

"Didn't know we had a musical celebrity in our midst, did you? John was the first man to play Elvis on the air. Quite an honor. Ask him to see his Elvis autograph sometime, or Elvis's first guitar." John's eyes are wide and horrified, so I backtrack. "Really, folks, he doesn't have any of that. He only wishes. Here's 'That's All Right,' big and bold on KZUK, 90.3 community radio."

Paige's eyes are so wide her eyebrows are in her hair. "John has Elvis's first guitar?"

John jumps up and comes for my throat with both hands. "You gotta learn to shut up!" I don't think he's joking.

"You told me to tell stories, so I told a story."

"Not like that!" He's on his way out the door for a cigarette and he flips me the bird over his shoulder.

"Sorry!" And I am. That was dumb. But if he was really mad he'd have picked up his music and walked home.

Paige is still amazed. "He could sell that for a zillion dollars."

The rest of the show is solid, and I'm pleased. I even let Paige talk, but all she says is "Uh ... hi." My request to the Ugly Children Brigade—all 27 of them—is to construct an Elvis statue somewhere. It was all I could think of. Maybe they'll make an Elvis mop.

When the show is over and Marijane is digging, digging, digging, we pack up our crap and head out to the parking lot—where we're met by Jason and Scream.

I want to run but I hold my ground.

John looks at them, then at me. "Are these guys for real?"

Jason looks me over. "So what's under there? You got a pussy under there, Gabe?"

"We're just heading to the car, all right?" I try to walk past them, but Scream grabs my arm and pulls me toward Jason, who stinks like beer. He's not so steady on his feet when he reaches out for me, and I pull back, but Scream's grip is relentless.

Paige is screeching. "Get your hands off him, asshole!"

Jason grabs my head and pushes it to his crotch. "Want some of this? Come on, Liz, you like dick, don't you? Or do you have one?" He grinds, trying to push my face into his fly. I try to bite him, but he yanks my head up, then pushes it down again. When I try to turn my head away from his crotch, Scream forces it back. Back to the bulge that's there.

I can barely hear John, but he's hollering. "Get the hell out of here!"

Jason keeps talking. "Not so much fun to pretend when someone calls you on it, huh? Where's that dick, Liz?" He's breathing hard.

Then Scream yanks my pants down and my shirt up, and Jason laughs. "Oooh, look at this! Boxers! There has to be a dick under there somewhere." Scream grabs my crotch, squeezing the Mango. "Holy fuck, what's that?" He squeezes again.

John's voice: "Walk away, dipshit, before you hurt someone or I bust your head in."

Jason's voice, ugly and hard. "You're a girl, not a fucking guy. Get it in your head, and keep to your fucking self. Stay away."

Stay away from what? Then there's a punch to my ear and everything's underwater. When my arm is released, I crumble to the pavement.

"Fuck you, stupid assholes!" Paige's voice.

"You think we won't fuck you up, too?" Scream's voice. I sit up a little and watch as she walks toward them.

"You're stupid cowards who can't own it." She's winding up now. "Or can you? Masks off, right now. You're gonna get your asses kicked by an old man and a girl!"

"Watch your back, bitch. We're seriously going to fuck with you AND It." Jason's going to hurt her, right here and now.

John again: "Paige, be quiet. You're not helping."

"Right here, chickenshits." Paige is glaring like she can knock them down with her eyes. "Or can't you handle it? Figure it out. I'll wait."

All she's doing is making it worse, and I'm gonna freak if she doesn't quit yelling. I get to my knees, then my feet.

"COWAAAAAAAAAAAAAAARDS! CHICKEN SHIIIIIIIIIIIIIITS!"

John grabs her. "Shut up!"

"No. They think they can stop him from being Gabe, and they can't. COWAAAAAARDS!"

John drags her by the arm to his car, where I've managed to stumble. "We're going to the police station. This is enough."

I hear footsteps running away, and a car starting.

Paige is next to me, face beet red. "God, Gabe, are you okay?" She gives me a hug like she hasn't seen me for years.

"Holy shit, that hurts."

"Sorry, oh god, sorry." She backs away, eyes wet.

John checks me over. "We have to go to the cops."

"No ... please." I can't talk very well.

He's touching my arms, my hair, checking for blood with gentle hands. "You have no choice. They assaulted you."

"Not ... going ... to matter."

"Fine." John steps back from me. "You're banned from my house as well as my collection and I'm going to cancel your show. Russ will listen to me."

"You wouldn't ... you can't." I can't believe he said that.

"Try me."

When I look at his face, really look, I see all the sadness from the afternoon combined with an incredible anger.

"John's right. We need the cops." Paige's arm is tight around my shoulders. Both of them are glaring at me, though Paige is still sniffling.

"Fine."

Paige helps me into John's car and he drives us to the police station. We make a report about Jason and Scream and what just happened. I even show them the Facebook page.

The officer who talks to us is polite but distant. Another officer stands in the corner of the room and scowls the entire time. He asks one question: "So you're … a dude … but you're still sort of a girl?" After I nod, his lip curls into a permanent sneer and stays that way for the rest of the time we're there. The polite officer promises to check into it.

I turn to John and Paige once we're in the car. "Satisfied?" I can talk better now, though my head is killing me.

"Yes. Let's go home." John starts the car.

"The cops will never find them. They'll never try."

"You don't know that." He sounds more convinced than I feel.

We drop Paige off and head back home after she's hugged me a million times and told me how sorry she is. John hauls his Elvis stuff out and turns to go, but then turns back. "You're the only family I've got. You and your folks and Pete. I have to take care of you, all right?"

I can't refuse him. "Okay."

"Besides that, you'd never jeopardize your music fix. Am I right?" Finally I see John's regular grin, despite the sad, sad look in his eyes.

"Night, John."

"Night, Gabe."

At noon, when my mom comes to knock, I tell her I'm sick. Then I lie on my bed and think about whether or not

I want to be Gabe. One part of my brain is screeching *NO NO NO NO NO*, over and over again. Finally, Elvis clears his throat in my head.

The *NO NO NO* voice is still screeching. But I let Elvis respond.

You only get one life, he says. *The answer is yes.*

I take a nap to get Elvis to shut up.

After I make myself eat some supper, I mix my Vibe show a little bit, rearranging a couple things we chose in our all-night session. It's not bad, but it's not perfect yet. I even chat a little, just to practice, but I feel stupid.

My arm is killing me where Scream had it, and my scalp too.

Then my phone beeps:

Srsly. Just the way u r. Hook up?

No.
Way.

I don't think I ever got the concept of butterflies in the stomach until this very second. Now it's the same as at the graduation party—if I had a dick, it would be hard right now. So hard I would have to make it un-hard, and it would take less than thirty seconds.

The best moment of my life is less than twenty-four hours after the worst one.

I can't answer her right now.

I go downstairs and watch TV with Pete, but I can't

sit still. I eat some leftovers. I walk around the block. My imaginary dick is still hard.

I can't think about this.

Around nine, I check Facebook, even though I almost don't want to. But I need to see if the Ugly Children Brigade has Elvis sculpture photos. There are 31 members now, which is up a few people, and someone posted two pictures at five this morning. The first one is a ten-foot tower of scrap wood and folding chairs with four velvet Elvis paintings draped on it, one on each side of the tower. Where the hell did they get velvet Elvis paintings in the middle of the night, let alone four of them? Someone else in this town must be Elvis's biggest fan.

The second one is more like the seed art my mom always dragged me to see at the state fair. It's flat on the ground, like in a dirt parking lot or something, and it's ten feet long and at least five feet wide. Elvis's hair looks like it's made of shredded rubber tires. His face is made of something that might be spread-out creamed corn. I can't quite tell what his eyes and nose are made of, but his mouth is made of flower petals, and it's a big smile. It's insanely strange, but totally cool.

On the ground underneath the Elvis face is a sign on a huge posterboard:

HATERS HAVE BEEN BLOCKED.
COME HANG WITH US AT THE B SIDE WALL!
1:30 A.M., JULY 9. WE WANT TO MEET YOU!

With a big smiley face.

That's about three weeks from today. The UCB wants to meet me in three weeks. That glow stick is back in my chest.

Three weeks is a long freaking time. Why not next week? Then again, who cares? These people made a graffiti wall for me. I'll do whatever they tell me.

But before the post of the pictures, before the haters were blocked, there's a post from Jason from two a.m.:

We're coming for IT.
    Know it.
    Believe it.
    Feel it.
    Kill IT.
    Smash IT.
    Stomp IT.
    Grind IT.
    We're coming for IT.
    Someday.
    Someday soon.

Scream commented on Jason's post: Fucking A.

My imaginary balls have crawled back into my body. Then it's hard to breathe, like really hard, and I have to lie down on my floor because the room is spinning around.

When I finally get up, I take a screen shot of each threat and print them all out so I can stick them in my scrapbook. Isn't that what a scrapbook is for—to record memories? This shit is certainly a memory.

And if I need to sue their asses, I have evidence.

Then, all of a sudden, I'm completely exhausted.

When I'm done brushing my teeth, I listen out the window to see what John's playing tonight. More Elvis.

Then I collapse into bed. My brain, of course, does not.

Maybe it's a trap. Maybe the UCB will toss me around in front of the B side wall and invite Jason and his buddy Scream to finish me off.

Or—maybe—they really want to meet me.

I weigh the questions, but no answer appears. And Elvis has nothing more to say. When it gets hard to breathe again, I chant in my head: *It's all right. It's all right.* I have John. I have Paige. I have my show. It's all right.

And Heather Graves wants me. The way I am.

My imaginary dick is hard again.

LADY GAGA IS THE NEW ELVIS BECAUSE SHE'S GOT A CRAZY WARDROBE, TOO

Monday. Paige says she's dying to go to Valleyfair, so I give in. And it's cheap on Mondays. Not that I really want to be thrown around by G forces or eat crappy food, but it's okay. I need to do something without scary guys in masks or sexy texts. Heather's not exactly blowing up my phone, but she's persistent, so I'm leaving my phone in the car.

Me. A guy with a Mango. Two girls on the radar. This is not my life.

As soon as we get there, Paige immediately wants to do the Power Tower, which is this humongous needle-looking thing where you sit in these open seats—with harnesses, of course, but still—and you get dragged up to the top. Then you fall. Forever.

Paige screams all the way down, but I don't make a sound.

"Oh my god, that was fun. Let's do it again!" She's out of breath and glowy from the adrenaline. Adorable.

I let myself look at her mouth for a few seconds before I answer her. "Not on your life."

"Come on, dude. Please?" She bats her eyes at me, just for effect.

"No way. Roller coasters, yes. That thing, never again."

She pouts for about five seconds, but then she pulls me off to the High Roller, which is an old wooden roller coaster that rattles and shakes, and that's scary enough. I don't throw up, but my stomach isn't ready for lunch after that.

We walk around and look at all the people. There are kids and parents, people on dates, and old couples walking very slowly. One kid is having a temper tantrum by the popcorn cart, complete with kicking his legs and screaming at the top of his lungs. His parents are standing next to him looking annoyed, and his big sister is standing over him, saying, "Josh, look, if you get off the ground, we can go to the Ferris Wheel. Come on, huh? This is boring." The parents catch us laughing, and they glare.

B96, a huge Top 40 station from the Cities, is doing live remote spots to promote the station and provide "the everyday sounds of your life" to Valleyfair-goers. Paige doesn't want to, but I make her stand there and watch the DJ for half an hour. I try to memorize how he interacts with people, how he makes eye contact and jokes with the huge crowd around him. He's totally relaxed and cool. He's probably been doing it for years. I ask Paige for a piece of paper and a pen, which she fishes out of her purse with a *you are so strange* look, and I take some notes. If it was just me and the Vibe managers, I'd be fantastic, but the crowd will be the scary thing. Not to mention the fact that Jason and Scream could be hiding somewhere.

While we're walking to find some food, I start imagining our next trip to Valleyfair. This fall we'll be in the Cities for good, her for school, me for work, so we can take time off, right? Just a little break. Maybe once in the fall and once in the spring. A long day of rides and goofing off. Then, when we're tired, we'll go home to the same apartment, make supper, and fall into bed. Together.

"Hey. Wake up." She yanks on my hand and I snap back.

"Just thinking."

It's so strange: Paige has been holding my hand for the entire day. Like we're a couple.

By two p.m., we're hot and sweaty. It must be 95 degrees in the shade.

Paige gives me a look. "Are you sure we can't go on the water rides?" She even wore her swimsuit, though I refused.

"Trans guys and water don't mix."

"No more Power Tower either?" She sticks out her lower lip to emphasize the pouty tone.

"Nope."

"How about bumper cars? Or will that hurt your delicate little head?"

"I'm gonna smash the crap out of you for saying that." So we get in line, then give each other whiplash for three minutes, then get in line to do it again. Josh the tantrum thrower and his big sister are in line too.

Then Paige looks at her phone. "We should go. I have to work tonight." She holds my hand all the way to the parking lot, then while we're driving. Not full hand-holding this time, but her pinky is hooked onto mine.

"What's up with the hand-holding?"

"What? Nothing." She pulls her hand away and looks out the window. "You don't like it?"

"No, I love it, it's just…you've never done that before."

"It seemed like the thing to do." She looks at me and shrugs. "That's all."

I hook my pinky back over hers. I don't have to think about Jason or Scream or Heather or the Vibe or anything. I just have to hold her pinky.

I check my phone after I drop her off. Twelve texts from Heather. I read them, but I don't answer.

Wednesday afternoon. I call Paige. "You want to club tonight? Or maybe Thursday?" I'm trying to think of more stuff to do to take my mind off everything, and I don't want to practice too much or it'll get stale. Plus I want to hold her hand some more.

Silence on the other end for a few seconds. "Maybe."

"You've got big plans? A replacement for Bobby X?"

Silence on the other end again.

"Paige, what's wrong?" Paige always talks. When she doesn't, something's up.

"Just ... I'll call you later, okay?" And she hangs up.

I have no idea. Sometimes she gets in a mood.

Six o'clock. I call Paige. "Why haven't you called me?"

Silence.

"Paige?"

"I'll call you in a few days, okay? It's ... I need to be alone right now." And she clicks off.

She's never said that before in the history of our relationship.

Thursday. I call her house, because she's not answering her cell, and her mom tells me she's at the mall with Allison and Marta. I try her cell again, and it goes to voicemail.

Friday night. John almost didn't let me come by myself, but I showed him my can of mace and my new pocket knife, and he relented. I need to be alone, because tonight is a Prince show. I know some people hate him but his music is timeless, old-school and new all at the same time. He's also a Minnesota son, so I think he deserves a show. But Prince is all about sex, so my imaginary dick is twitching again. I don't need John around while my mind's in the gutter.

Paige always admires Prince's fashion sense, starting with the thigh-high leather stiletto boots and no visible pants of any kind in his "Controversy" video. When he does wear clothes, he's quite dashing, especially in his tailored suits. But a few years ago he wore pink pants to the Academy Awards. Please.

My mind is too unfocused to be doing this. All I see is Paige stretched out on my bed. She still hasn't called me back. Sometimes that vision is replaced by Heather at the graduation party. But Paige comes in and shoos her away.

"Welcome, welcome, to Beautiful Music for Ugly Children on 90.3 community radio, KZUK, and welcome, dear Ugly Children Brigade. Thank you for the Elvises last week. How did you manage to find that many shredded tires—or that many Velvet Elvis paintings? I want to know who those belong to. For those of you who are new, I'm Gabe, and today is a Prince show. First piece of trivia: Prince is the name on his birth certificate. And here's 'I Feel for You,' made popular by Chaka Khan's remake, but written by the Small Sexy One."

This is even worse than the seduction show. I try to keep my brain in useful territory, and I put more songs on and take them off, all the while chatting about Prince trivia. Then I see Paige, clubbing in the Cities, looking sweaty and adorable.

My phone beeps with another text:

Want 2 hook up? Answer me. :)

Sproing. Imaginary dick in action. I respond:

On the air. U r not listening?

Then I almost miss my cue. "So, Beautiful Children, we can't deny Prince is amazingly erotic, his looks *and* his music, and no, saying Prince is erotic doesn't make me want to have sex with a man. He's a pretty small dude—not very noticeable when he's being a regular guy. But when he's onstage and the energy gets going, I know people in the audience look around and say, 'hey, you're cute, wanna bone?' to whoever's standing next to them. I've never actually seen it happen, but I bet it does." Then I decide to throw caution out the studio window. "Okay, I'm tempting the FCC with this one, but here's 'Sexy MF,' going out to the texter."

Hopefully she's listening now. The song has enough "motherfuckers" in it to get the station fined seven times over, but I can't imagine the FCC is listening.

I wish those texts were from Paige.

The song growls onto the air, and I start thinking about body parts mashing together in the dark. I can't contemplate having sex, imaginary dick or not. A guy with breasts can't have sex. Can he? Maybe sex is fine between two people who love each other. Maybe love's enough. No matter what body parts you have, or don't have, or wish you had.

There's nobody stupid enough on this planet to think

those last two statements could be true, and I've got to be the only person in Maxfield who graduated from high school as a virgin.

I almost miss my cue again. "Did you know that Prince actually performed on *American Bandstand*, that late great musical TV show? Here's 'Soft and Wet,' definitely not one of the songs he did for Dick Clark. By the way, Ugly Children, what do you think you could decorate with condoms? I wouldn't get the lubricated kind, if I were you."

Lots more music, then a little more talk. "When you think about it, maybe Prince is sexy because he's in the middle—those big brown eyes and long lashes, plus he used to have that long wavy hair. But he's got plenty of muscles and testosterone. Let's call him a birl. Or a gir-man. People still like him, whoever and whatever he is. He even did the Super Bowl halftime show, and if that's not the ultimate American endorsement of somebody's music, I'm clueless."

I check the CD again. "To close the show with a bang, no pun intended, let's do 'Musicology' and 'Black Sweat,' some of the very modern old-school funk grooves from his more recent discs. Can't wait for the pics, Ugly Children. I'll see you next week. This is Gabe, and you've been listening to Beautiful Music for Ugly Children right here on KZUK, community radio 90.3."

I should become a priest. That would solve the whole sex issue. Too bad I'm not Catholic. Paige is, so maybe she'd know someone I could ask. But what would they do when they found tampons in my room?

The ache in my crotch has transferred itself to my head.

After I get home, I try to call Paige.

" … Hello?" She's asleep.

"Why haven't you called me back?"

" … Liz?" Then she gasps. "I mean Gabe! Gabe!" Then there's silence.

"What the hell is wrong with you?"

"I'll call you tomorrow, okay?" And the line goes dead.

I try to be mad at her, but I'm just sad.

T-PAIN IS THE NEW ELVIS BECAUSE HE'S ON A BOAT, MOTHERBEEPERS, AND ELVIS PROBABLY WANTED A BOAT, TOO

Thursday afternoon, eight days since the first "I'll call you back" never happened. I've tried everything from messages at her house, texts, stalking Video Rewind, and bombing the wall of her Facebook page, but she's never anywhere, and never able to talk if she accidentally answers her phone.

I'm dying inside.

Chris has been patient with me because I've been worrying about Jason/Scream/Paige, not always in that order, and practicing my Vibe show, but he says I've got to get it together or he's firing me, no joke. As I'm getting in my car to go to McSwingy's, John comes out of his house and waves at me.

"Just a few days and you'll be king of the airwaves! You gotta do your Vibe set for me tonight, okay? All the way through, music and words."

"Yeah."

"No lukewarm 'yeahs' allowed—this is big!"

I blurt it all out in a big rush. "Paige is mad at me."

"Why?"

"She won't tell me." The tears are threatening but I shove them back.

"Her loss." He shrugs.

"It's my loss."

He pats my shoulder. "Girls come and go, you know."

"Not this one." My voice is barely above a whisper.

"You may love her to her core, but you can't let her get in your way. You're on your way to a whole new life. New job, new friends, new city. New history." He gives me a look that would stop a train, then heads back towards his house again.

John's right. Even about Paige. And I hate that fact.

Elvis in my head: *It will be all right, Gabe.*

Me: *Shut up, fool. You don't know a single goddamn thing.*

When I get to McSwingy's, Chris is standing in the back of the store, digging through the vinyl racks like he's a prairie dog.

I get *ANGELA* pinned on and wander over. "Somebody buried treasure in here?"

Chris holds up *Let it Bleed*. He's *MR. SNUFFLEUPAGUS* today. "When I was in college, I sailed a copy of this at a pretty girl, from our balcony onto hers, and I knocked her beer all over her lap." He hugs the album to his chest. "You must never throw a Stones album as a Frisbee."

I grab a copy of *The Marvelous Sonny and Cher*. "This, on the other hand, could be used as a Frisbee, a dinner plate, or a dog poop scoop."

Chris takes Sonny and Cher from me and flings the album across the room, where it slices into a display of Bob Dylan CDs with a large crash. "Whoops." But Chris is grinning. "Shall we thin the vinyl inventory today, Gabe? Maybe after you get Bob off the floor? Sorry about that."

I gather up the Dylan CDs and stack them into a nice neat display while Chris starts digging through for choice flinging material. "Look at this! *Neon Eighties Hits. Best of the Carpenters. Tone Loc Goes Mellow. The New York Philharmonic plays Sixties Hippie Tunes. K-Tel Disco Hits of the Seventies.*"

"Let's rescue that last one." I grab it from his hands to examine the album cover. "No disco should be discarded."

"Your Prince show was good, by the way." Chris keeps digging. "It takes balls to play 'Sexy MF' on the radio, even in the midnight hour."

I bop Chris on the head with *K-Tel Disco Hits of the Seventies*. "You listen? Why the hell didn't you tell me?"

"I'm even a member of the UCB."

"You are?"

"I was number 33." Which means the number's gone up again.

We dig some more and find *Mr. Rogers' Christmas Album*, *Sergio Mendes Plays You to Sleep*, and *Henry Mancini Does Detroit*, plus about two dozen others not worth saving.

Then Paige comes in and the whole world stops.

"Uh … hi. Paige." It's like I'm looking at a mermaid, I'm so surprised.

"Hi." She's so tense her shoulders are up by her ears. "Can we talk?"

"Chris, I'm going outside with Paige for a sec, okay?"

He dismisses me with a wave, though he gives Paige a flirty smile. "Just don't be long."

Paige and I head outside, the bell above the door jingling as we go. Once we're out, she walks down the sidewalk about ten feet, then turns around to look at me. "Why does your nametag say Angela?"

"Because it does, and I'm not going to chase you, so if you want to talk, you have to come back here."

She takes one step closer to me. "I know I've been a complete bitch."

I realize I'm standing there with my arms crossed, looking like a bastard myself, so I uncross them. "I agree." I want to say, *Where the hell have you been, I've been out of my mind, don't ever ever do that again!* But I restrain myself.

"It was just … " Suddenly she's flung herself into my arms and she's bawling her head off. We stand like that for a minute, and I comfort her as best I can. The sobs are shaking her whole body. Then she realizes she's buried herself in my chest, so she backs up a couple feet and swipes at her face. "I...um...that was...sorry. What time do you get off?"

I can't think for a second. "Nine."

"I'll meet you at the Hag, okay? We can talk then." Now she sounds a little more like Paige. "I'll explain, I promise." She's wiping under her eyes, making sure she's gotten all the runny mascara out from under them.

"I guess." I don't know what else to say.

"See you then." She gives me a little wave and heads toward the Hag. I can see it from where we're standing.

What the hell just happened?

I go back inside and start sorting through the promo posters. Chris is done with the vinyl, and he gives me a curious look but doesn't say anything. For some reason, I exchange *ANGELA* for *BETTY*.

The bell above the door jingles, but I don't look up. A girl comes up to me and tosses her hair. "Do you have the new Decemberists CD?"

"Right over here." I guide her to its spot.

Chris picks up the stack of worthless vinyl. "I'm going to clutter up a few more square feet of floor space." He heads off with his records into the mess that is the back room.

I continue my dig through the box of promo stuff. I pull out a poster from Gwen Stefani and study it. Paige really does remind me of her. Then I find a gift straight from the music gods: *Oh No It's Devo*, an actual album cover, square and perfect. I have no idea how it got into this box, but I don't care. It's not even creased. I set it aside for contemplation, because it needs a place of honor.

"I was hoping you'd be here." A voice from behind me.

Good Jesus, please, not now.

Heather puts a Drake CD on the counter. "How are you?"

"Just fine." Get organized, brain. Smile. Act happy to see her. "That'll be $10.95."

She's got her hair tucked up in one of those messy buns, a few pieces swirling around her face and showing off her big brown eyes. Her huge purse is purple, and it matches her tank top. Not quite as amazing as at the graduation party, but close.

She flips through her purse, hands me a twenty, and I give her nine bucks and a nickel, then put her CD in a bag. Her lips tilt into a smile. "Thanks for the dedication the other night. Pretty hot."

"Um ... sure. You're welcome."

Then she glances at my nametag. "You've given up on Gabe? Betty's okay too."

Now her friend's at the counter, and she hands me a Decemberists CD. We exchange money. The friend looks at Heather, then at me, then frowns. "I'll see you outside." *Ding ding ding* goes the door.

Heather's still studying me, looking coy and cute—and steady. She knows what she wants. "So, are you interested?"

I can barely answer. "Um, yeah, but ..." A million images run through my mind: Heather's breasts hair amazing mouth on a couch in a car making out I'm touching oh I'm touching she's touching no fear no fear no fear ... "I sort of ... can't. Right now." At some point, I'll have to give up on Paige. But not yet.

"Oh ... well ... okay." I don't think she's used to being told no. She tosses her hair and turns to leave. "If you change your mind, text me." She smiles over her shoulder, like a TV commercial, but she doesn't really go towards the door.

"Thanks for shopping at McSwingy's." I smile one more time, because it's my job to smile.

Heather frowns, since I didn't do what she wanted, and the door jingles as she huffs out. Once she's gone, I collapse onto the stool behind the counter. The chatter in my brain is intense—it's Heather and Paige, and they're pacing and flailing their arms and yelling at me. Then Mara joins in and the noise gets really loud.

I just turned down the hottest girl ever. What is wrong with me?

The next few hours go by about as fast as the first eighteen years of my life, but finally I make it to the Hag. Even though it's almost dark, Paige is sitting outside. The rest of the patio is deserted. I hustle inside, grab some coffee, and hustle back out.

Paige is nervous, picking at the edge of the table and moving her frappuccino glass around. "We really need to talk."

"Duh." I sit down. "Where the hell have you been?"

"Have you got your show ready for the Vibe?"

"Changing the subject doesn't work. You dropped out of my life and I want to know why." I'm pissed, which doesn't compliment her agitation. We face each other, arms crossed.

She can't return my stare for long. "I ..."

"Get to the goddamn point!" My brain is buzzing. "What happened?"

"They found me."

"Who?"

"Jason and Scream. They came to Video Rewind." I can see the tears on her face again. "Such big chickens, with their masks."

"What did they do?" My ugliness has now spilled onto Paige.

"Yelled and pushed me. Frank called the cops and kicked them out." Frank is her manager.

"Did they hurt you?"

"They pushed me into a display case." She shows me the bruises on her left arm.

"What did they say?"

"Stupid stuff. What they said on the UCB page, just with me included. 'We're gonna kill you too, bitch,' blah blah blah."

What do you say when your best friend is attacked because of you? Not even *by* you, *because of* you?

I'm gonna black out, so I put my head between my knees.

"I'll say I'm sorry every day for the rest of our lives, okay? I just ... god. I'm sorry."

"Gabe?"

"What?" I stare at the cement and my feet. The panic passes. A little.

"Look at me." She doesn't sound mad.

When I pull my head back up, she's staring. "Gonna puke?"

"Not now." I don't think.

Paige looks away. "I'm sorry, too."

"For what?"

She pauses for a long time. "They made me think about it."

Not what I was expecting. "Think about what?" I move my chair closer to hers. I need to touch her, even if we're in public. Her hand, her arm, anything.

She pulls away before I get close enough. "What Gabe means. To us."

"What do you mean, 'what he means, to us'? He's not someone else."

"That's why I didn't call you." She pulls her feet up into the chair seat and wraps her arms around her knees. "I had to decide what I wanted to do."

My head explodes.

"What you wanted to *do*? What the fuck did they say to you?" I cannot believe what's coming out of her mouth. "What the fuck was that scene outside McSwingy's five hours ago if you didn't know what you wanted to do?" I stand up and shove my chair to the opposite side of the table, as far away from her as possible. "What the hell could they say that you'd listen to?"

"Stuff like, 'You'll never get ahead with It for a friend. Everybody will hate you.'"

"That's never mattered to you before." I glare at her. "How many times have you stuck up for me?"

"Yeah, but ... you weren't Gabe before. You were still Liz."

This makes no sense. "So?"

Now she's very quiet. "Well ... people could think ... I'm messed up, too. Those assholes said nobody would invite me to parties, or want to be my roommate at school if I was hanging out with you." She won't look at me. "It matters ... to have lots of friends."

"Messed up?" I repeat. She is not saying this. "I'm messed up?"

"No, but ... "

"Lord knows we couldn't jeopardize your popularity now, but when you go to college, nobody's gonna know you anyway. It's a whole new life!"

"But if you meet my new friends, you might ... freak them out." She's embarrassed, which is good, because this is one complete bullshit reason to give up a friendship.

"You honestly care about your social standing more than you care about me?"

"It's very strange when your best friend says 'hey, I'm really a guy.'"

"That was MONTHS ago! And I tried to tell you in eighth grade. Remember?"

"Of course I remember. But being the target of violence isn't something that happens in your average friendship. And what if it happens again?"

All the fire goes out of me.

I go inside the Hag and get a glass of water. Then I carry it down the block to my car, because I don't know where else to go. But I don't get in—I walk around the block, still carrying the glass, which I almost put down so I can text Heather. But I don't. Before I take the glass back in, I remember to drink the water. When I come out to the patio, Paige is still sitting there, looking miserable.

I sit down and take a deep breath. "We've been friends since kindergarten. Through everything. You can't stop now."

If I lose her, I will die.

She's sniffling. "I know. Oreos, Harry Potter marathons, stupid dance and piano lessons. When I liked Sam Wilson and you'd hang up on him all the time for me. Tenth grade geometry when we got caught cheating on that test. Last year when you got food poisoning—so gross. And all over my car, too." Her mouth twists. "And now you're Gabe, with a whole new life, so there's no need for me. You'll find a whole new set of friends when you move away."

"We're both moving to the Cities!"

"But you're still going away." The tears are washing off what little makeup she had left after the crying fit at McSwingy's.

I hand her a napkin from the table. "How am I going away if you're going to be there, too?"

She wipes her nose, then her eyes. "You're not Liz anymore." Then she throws the napkin back at me. There's something else she's not saying. I can't figure it out, but I can see it behind the last few tears.

"How am I not the person you know, aside from my name? Did I ever, in the time you've known me, behave like a person named Liz might behave? Not to be stereotypical, but did I ever seem comfortable with makeup or dolls or dresses or my breasts or boyfriends or the idea of being a mom or talking forever on the phone or emotions?"

"No."

"Since I've made Gabe public, have I stopped liking music or Elvis or you? Have we stopped doing stuff together, or talking to each other almost every day?"

"No."

"So what's different about me?"

"Well … you have a Mango." There's still something more, but she's not saying it.

"Yes, I do, and it's right here on the patio with us. But I'm not going to stop being your friend because I have a Mango."

"What if you decide you only want trans friends?"

"Why would that happen? I'd love to have trans friends, but like I said, we've been friends since KINDERGARTEN, and I always assumed, silly me, that we'd be friends for a long time, like maybe forever."

She gives me a tiny smile. "Remember when we were in fourth grade and in different classrooms?"

"When we'd leave notes in the bathroom, and we'd run out of class every ten minutes to see if there was a new one?" In my mind I see a blonde girl with ribbons on her jeans racing down a school hallway. "I love you—way too much to give up on us."

Paige chokes on her frappuccino.

"Not like that!" Now I'm blushing. "As my best friend." My heart is doing flippy-flops.

Once she's recovered, she doesn't look me in the face. "You really just said that."

"Yeah, but..."

"Too bad. You're my slave for life."

"Whatever." For some reason, this feels way more serious than what happened on my bed.

She's still not looking at me. "I don't have your stamina."

"What stamina?"

"To do what you're doing."

"Sitting in a chair?"

"It takes so much to be Gabe. I'd fall apart in under a day."

"No you wouldn't."

More silence. I need to break it. "Thank you."

She shifts in her chair but finally looks at me. "For what?"

"For telling me all this. I'm just... incredibly sorry."

I have no idea if we're still friends. It could go either way.

"There's no way I could give you up." She reaches over and squeezes my hand. "Nobody else lets me dress them."

The door to the patio slams, and two girls come out, looking around for a table. Even in the growing darkness, I can tell that one is Mara, and she can tell it's me. She moves around to the other side of her friend, so she's farther away, and she whispers to her friend over the top of her iced mocha glass.

I lean across the table. "See that girl in the orange dress? That's Mara."

"Mara from the date?" Paige cranes around to look.

"Thanks for being subtle."

She turns back to me with a light in her eyes that's deeper than mischief. "Let's mess with her."

The electricity is humming, and she looks at me, really looks at me like she's never seen me before. If I'm imagining it right, the word on her forehead is YES. Then she half stands up, leans across the table, and plants the softest, sweetest kiss on my lips. It's like butterflies. Sunshine.

Heaven.

Then I hear a glass shatter and a door slam. When I open my eyes, Mara's friend is standing there, alone, with a bewildered look on her face. The iced mocha is on the ground.

Paige laughs, loud and hard. "Perfect!" She sits back down and we fist bump. But then she realizes what happened in the last thirty seconds and the electricity goes up 150 percent. "Do not expect me to do that ever again! That was just for Mara's sake!"

"We're still friends, right? Or are we friends with benefits now?" I can't resist.

She kicks me so hard my shin gets a goose egg.

I'll think about that kiss for a long, long time.

Friday midnight. This week's radio show is for Paige. John's in the corner, flipping my Zippo open and closed.

"Welcome, my friends, to Beautiful Music for Ugly Children on 90.3, KZUK. I'm Gabe, and today's show is for someone who's definitely not ugly, though she's part of the Ugly Children Brigade. Paige, this hour's for you and your ability to read all seven Harry Potter books in seventy-two hours."

She loves Stevie Wonder too, so I start with "Superstition" in the tricky CD player and say a little prayer over it. It hasn't jackknifed lately, so I hope the trend continues. Once the song starts, it stays steady.

The phone rings. John's ears perk up. "Maybe it's a girl!"

"Hello, KZUK, the Z that sucks."

Paige is pleased. I think. "Why is this show for me?"

"For helping me completely piss Mara off."

"That was a one-time deal."

"We can't add kissing to our list of things to do together?"

She ignores me. "Can I make a request?"

"If I have it."

"What's my all-time favorite song?" She thinks I won't know.

"Decent music or silly-ass?"

"Silly-ass."

"It's sitting right next to me. Dumbest song in the universe." It's a museum-quality example of dorky seventies music.

"My mom used to sing it at bedtime. Not like you care."

"Go read your textbook, brainiac."

"Whatever." She hangs up.

"Was it a girl?" John wants to know.

"Just Paige."

"She's still a girl. I'm going out to smoke." He takes my Zippo with him.

The songs keep flowing: Modest Mouse, trashy David Lee Roth Van Halen. Her tastes are almost as strange as mine.

"So, Ugly Children, I bet you have a friend or two that you lean on. Friends who are like cozy warm blankets on Minnesota winter nights. Or thick wool socks—we need those in this state. Music is my cozy warm blanket, but my friend Paige is my best pair of wool socks. Sorry, Paige, it's a strange analogy, but it's the only thing I can think of."

She's gonna kill me. I put on a song so I don't have to talk.

The phone rings again. John's back, and he's leaned his head against the wall, eyes closed. "You really are the chick magnet tonight, aren't you?"

I glare at him as I pick it up. "KZUK, the Z that sucks."

"You're so disgusting. You know you need to die, right?" The sounds hiss into my ear. "Let's settle it, huh? Tomorrow night."

I'm going to puke all over the phone. "You're challenging me to a duel?"

"How about your house, since we know where you live? Maybe your brother can help you. Or your parents?"

I try to keep my voice steady. "You do not get to fuck with my family, but come by around seven and I'll have Popsicles."

Click.

John can see my face. "Who the hell was that?"

"They threatened Pete and my folks."

"Cop shop after the show. You got it?" He points at me to make sure I hear him.

"Yeah."

Now I'm so jumpy I can't think. I call Paige back, just to feel a little more normal, even though I have nothing to say. "Hey, uh ... hi."

"I'm reading, dude. What do you want? I can't believe you said I was like wool socks."

"Uh ... you know how the UCB asked me to hang with them next week?" Of course she knows. She's mentioned it every day since the photo went up.

"You're not chickening out, aren't you? I told everybody you were coming!"

"You're going too, right?"

"Isn't your song almost over?"

I hang up and get my act together.

"All right, Ugly Children, where have your lips been tonight? Kissing friends? Kissing lovers? Kissing the statue of Merriweather Maxfield? Show me your lip prints—how many can you make? Let's see kiss prints all over town." Last week's challenge, to decorate with condoms, got exercised on the *WELCOME TO MAXFIELD* sign, complete with twisted dog balloons that weren't really balloons all over the grass in front of the sign. "To end today's show, here's a request from Paige herself. It's cheese wiener, total seventies easy listening music, but she wanted to hear it. This is community radio 90.3, KZUK, and you're listening to Beautiful Music for Ugly Children. Here's England Dan and John Ford Coley, 'Love is the Answer.'"

If love is the answer, what's the question?

Maybe it just matters that you know the answer. And believe it. Believe *in* it.

John and I go to the police station and tell them about the threat. They tell me they'll have someone come by my house tomorrow, and not to worry. I ask them to park a block down so my mom won't notice them. We'll see if they show. At least the cop who sneered wasn't there.

At this point, I'm just tired. Bring it on. Let's get it over with.

By two a.m., the UCB has posted their kissing pictures. Merriweather Maxfield is covered in lip prints—red—

while a huge pair of purple lips has been drawn in the parking lot of Food Pride, and the sign for our mall is covered in Xs and Os of pink chalk. There are also photos of faces covered in smooches—Jenna Hitchcock, with red lips and bright pink lip prints all over her cheeks, laughing with Brad Espenson, who's got bright pink lips and red lip prints all over him. In all my life, I never guessed I'd be one degree of separation away from Jenna Hitchcock and Brad Espenson. Those two wouldn't call 911 if Liz was lying bloody on the sidewalk. But Gabe? Evidently he's okay.

I drift off, imagining Paige. We're holding hands and kissing, and nobody's embarrassed or weird.

Maybe it's too outrageous.

Maybe it's possible.

Maybe I'll grow two more heads tomorrow.

That's what bites about the future—there's no way to predict it. You just have to show up and see what happens.

RUSH LIMBAUGH CAN'T BE THE NEW ELVIS; HE'S TOO MEAN

Saturday night. I get a phone call telling me that there will be an unmarked cop car half a block east of my house at six p.m., which surprises me. I'm even more surprised when they show up. At 6:45 I go outside and sit on my step.

When I was in eighth grade, I wanted to die.

I move fast, so Paige has to run.

"Liz, hold on!"

I don't slow down, and Paige is panting. The snow feels good on my face, but I ignore that fact and keep moving. It's cold, it's January, it's late at night.

Suddenly, it seems, we're on the bridge over the highway.

The cars whiz by underneath us, headlights making the snow dance in bright circles. I put one leg over so I'm straddling the guardrail.

"What the fuck are you doing?" Paige doesn't use that word, let alone scream it at top volume. My mom probably heard her since my house is only six blocks away.

"I wanted you to come because I want to say goodbye in person. No note this way. You can tell people."

"Move your leg!" Paige screams again and pulls on my shoulder.

"Back off, Paige! This is my suicide!" She moves about ten feet away.

"Why?" She is actually wringing her hands. I thought only people on TV did that.

"Why do you think?"

"I have no idea!" She's crying, and the tears are freezing on her face as fast as she cries them.

"What happened two months ago?" I slowly move my other leg over the top, so I'm sitting on the rail facing away from Paige. The rail is maybe a foot wide, and the ledge below me is maybe six inches wide. A boot would slip right off if I stood up. I lean back, not wanting to rush the situation. Cars are whizzing by under me. It might be seventy feet between me and them.

Paige's voice is a sobby shriek. "What the hell do you mean?"

"What life-changing event happened to you two months ago?"

I can hear her sniffle. "I don't know ... I got my period. So what?"

"And then what happened to me, since we're BFFs and we do everything together?"

"You got yours, too. What the fuck does that have to do with jumping off a bridge?" She wipes her nose with the back of her glove. "Get your ass over here! You're not doing this."

"Oh yes I am. What happened today?"

"We went to the Wow Zone!" She's sobbing again.

"What happened at the Wow Zone?"

"You played laser tag, you bowled, you played video games. So what? You…" Her voice trails off. Then she screams, "You got your period. So what?"

"Ugly, huge blood spots, all over the crotch of my jeans."

She's so confused. "It's just your period! Nobody saw but me!"

"What did they tell us in fifth grade health class—what does it mean to have your period?" I look down again as I ask the question. Those cars are really fast. There's no ice on the roads.

"You dumbass, it means you're a woman. What are you DOING?"

"Do you like being a woman?"

"I DON'T KNOW WHAT YOU'RE TALKING ABOUT!" Paige's voice tells me how high her panic level is.

I turn to look behind me. I can see she wants to come near me again, but she doesn't know how I'll take it. I turn back and look under my feet. Still lots of fast cars. "My body is lying, and it's so fucking gross." I keep staring down. "I'm not a woman." It wouldn't hurt, once I hit. I don't think.

She takes a deep, deep breath, and she doesn't yell. "Okay. You're not a woman. Can you come over here so we can talk about it?"

I turn around to look at Paige again. "Not at the moment."

"How long will you be on the ledge?"

"Until I decide whether I want to live or die."

"What if I help you fix it?"

"Fix what?"

"It's the twenty-first century. People can fix anything. There's got to be a way. But nobody can help you if you jump." She puts her hands on her hips and cocks her head at me.

She has a point.

I turn back around and look down at the cars again, then I wiggle my leg a tiny bit, pushing my boot out over the ledge below me. Gravity works. It would be easy.

"You'd help me?"

"Yes." She sounds more like herself.

"We're thirteen."

"We won't be thirteen forever."

Another good point.

I pull one leg back to the bridge side so I'm straddling the guardrail. "How can you help me?"

I hear Paige exhale and sob at the same time. "I don't know! I'll figure it out. Just come over here by me."

I pull the other leg over, stand up, and walk to Paige. She collapses into me, hugging me with all her might. "Liz, oh god, holy shit…" She can't say any more.

I don't shed a tear. I just hold her.

Finally she looks at me. "Please don't do that again, or I will kick your ass."

"You're just a skinny girl. What can you do?"

"I can take you." She probably can.

We walk back to my house, very slowly, because I ache all over. The snow is falling fast, and the tracks we made on the way to the bridge are gone.

"Liz...?" Paige hesitates. "What do you mean, you're not a woman?"

"I don't know how to explain it."

She puts her hand on my arm. "What if I can't find a way to fix it?"

I move faster. "Then it can't be fixed."

"We can Google it."

"Not tonight."

We walk a little more.

"I really will help you."

I glare at her. "You can start by shutting up."

"I wasn't going to tell anyone."

We get home, and no one's even noticed we were gone. Mom and Dad are watching a movie and throwing popcorn at each other, and Pete is in bed. We take off our winter gear and go upstairs. When we finally shut off the light, Paige tosses and turns in her sleep, and I shiver all night long, like I'm still on the bridge.

I never brought it up after that night, and neither did Paige. We just tried to pretend it didn't happen.

John joins me at seven o'clock with a box of Popsicles. We eat two Popsicles apiece and have a music argument about the Sex Pistols—who was better, Johnny Rotten or

Sid Vicious? We decide Vicious was cooler, but Rotten had more talent.

No sign of Jason and Scream by nine p.m., so we go inside after the cops drive away.

I hope they don't kill me. Things are just getting good.

Tuesday afternoon. Paige wants to go shopping. When I get in her car, she looks out the window, not at me. "Did you bring money?"

"No. Why?"

"We're dressing you up too. Where's your ATM card?"

"Lost in my room."

Paige sighs. "I'll spot you. You'll want to look good for the Vibe, plus the UCB when you meet them." She still hasn't glanced my way.

"Okay, but I refuse to go to Hollister, just so you know. And why aren't you looking at me?"

She turns to me so I'll lay off, but her eyes focus on my hair, not on my face. Then she turns back to watch the road. "No reason."

Her voice is cool as a cucumber, but her fingers are tapping the steering wheel. Paige has never been good at hiding her anxiety.

"Are you going to stop being my friend again? If that's true, shopping is out."

"I'm driving here. Stop talking." Tap tap tap on the steering wheel.

"Whatever you say."

Paige wants accessories today—scarves, bracelets, earrings—so we head to the mall, where you can still see pink Xs and Os on the sign. We start at Target, of course. I browse in the men's section and decide on a T-shirt with a Ramones logo on it. It's not too tight, and that's key, because it means my binder won't show. But can I really meet the UCB wearing a T-shirt everyone will know is from Target? Don't I need to look cooler than that?

I meet Paige up front and we pay for our stuff—she loans me ten for the shirt. Then we walk for what seems like miles to the other end of the mall so we can hit Victoria's Secret. I sit on a bench outside, facing away from the window displays. Too much information. Then we're all over the place, including American Eagle, Hot Topic, and Claire's. My skin almost crawls from all the estrogen in Claire's, but Paige is in her element, and of course there are a zillion accessories that capture her attention.

She's still not looking at me. She looked at my new shirt, the shoes I tried on in Payless—very manly loafers—and a wallet I showed her in Hot Topic. But she hasn't met my eyes once.

Finally we're in the food court to grab a soda. She's still buying, since I have no money.

"Mountain Dew or Pepsi?" No eye contact.

"Pepsi. And if you don't look me in the face, I'm going to throw it at you."

This gets her attention. "Don't you dare. I just bought this scarf." She stalks by me. "Let's go home."

Once we're in her car, I grab the keys just as she's going for the ignition. "What the hell is your issue?"

"Nothing." Paige is rummaging in her purse, looking for a spare set of keys. Finally she stops and looks at me. "We kissed."

"I know that." I try not to look too pleased.

"You are my BFF, not my boy FF."

"Couldn't they be one and the same?" When the words are out, I wish I could suck them back into my mouth, because the imaginary word on her forehead is NO, followed by a hundred exclamations points. "Okay, never mind, just kidding."

"You'd better be." More silence. She stares at an older lady crossing in front of the car. "It's just not ... part of who we are."

She has no idea how sad that statement is, but I make sure not to show it. "Okay. Fine. Now will you quit being so bitchy?"

"Yes. Can I have my keys back?" She holds out her hand, still looking at me, which is a good sign.

"Here."

"Let's go to the Cities. I really want you to have something nice for the UCB. Let them think you have a turntable, all that. You do have a Mango."

I have to be at work at four, and it's already eleven. "It's gotta be quick."

"I'll speed." She puts the car in gear. "I know a great boutique in Uptown. Not too trendy, not too spendy." Her perky self is back, and that's good. The tense Paige is just too awful.

We spend an hour in Rampage, and she makes me try on shirt after shirt. Finally we find a nice button-up one in a very cool purple color—"dusky plum," she says, like I would have any idea—and a very cool pair of jeans. It costs a heap, but McSwingy's has helped the savings account. And it's worth it to look good for the big stuff. Paige is generous enough to share her credit card with me, but she makes me swear I'll pay her tomorrow.

She drops me at McSwingy's. "Have a good shift."

I'd better make sure, once and for all. "No boyfriend/ girlfriend?"

"End of story." But she doesn't look me in the eye. So it's not really the end. Good. It's her turn to be confused.

"Call my mom and tell her to pick me up at nine, will you? I forgot my phone, too."

Paige rolls her eyes. "Loser." Then she drives away, taking my dreams with her.

Paige must have called, because someone's parked and waiting for me after work. But it's not my mom—it's my dad. "How was your shift?"

"Decent." He's putting himself out there, so I'll reciprocate. "I sold three Eric Clapton vinyl reprints."

He's surprised. "There's Clapton vinyl?"

"Just reissued."

"Put me down for one. I'll have to find my turntable."

"We have a turntable?" I had no idea.

"Somewhere in the attic." He chuckles. "Surprised you haven't found it by now."

Then it hits me. "I forgot a Father's Day gift, didn't I? That's pretty crappy. The album's on me."

He doesn't look at me. "It's okay."

"I'm sorry."

He lets it go. "When I was in college, they used to have classic rock laser light shows on Friday nights at the campus planetarium. At the Clapton one there was a stoned guy in the back who yelled 'Sunshine of Your Love'! in between the songs until they played it, then he started yelling for 'Freebird.' Some other dude yelled 'That's not Clapton!' and he yelled back 'So what?'" He chuckles.

"Did they play 'Freebird'?"

"I don't remember. Hey, want to stop and get a Blizzard?" We're driving by the Dairy Queen, so my dad slows down and actually engages my eyes with his.

"Sure." I think he was expecting me to say no.

We order and take our Blizzards outside to sit with the crowd at the picnic tables. Dad sees some people he works with and wanders over to talk to them. I'm perfectly content to sit and observe. Some guy bought his girlfriend an ice cream cone, but before he gives it to her he tries to stuff it in her bikini top. Then it drips on her breast and he licks it off.

Please.

Then I hear my dad yell, "Hey!" When I look up, he's

motioning to me, so I walk over, praying things won't be horrible.

He puts his hand on my shoulder. "Let me introduce you to the Millers. They're our biggest clients. Bob, Evelyn, this is my..." He breathes as deeply as he can. "This is Gabe."

I almost can't stick out my hand to shake Bob's, but I do, and I manage a smile at the same time. "Nice to meet you, Bob."

Bob looks me up and down but doesn't miss a beat. "Your dad tells us you've just graduated. Any college plans?" Bob's very slick and smooth, the kind of guy I couldn't be if I tried a million times. Just like I couldn't be the boob-licking dude.

"Still working on it."

Evelyn chimes in. "Maybe you should go into accounting like your dad." She gives my dad a big grin, sort of a *he's a chip off the old block, isn't he?* kind of grin.

"I haven't decided."

"Good luck!" Evelyn turns back to her own Blizzard as I realize mine's now a cup of soup. Bob and my dad shake hands one more time and my dad guides me back to our car by my elbow, just like he did when I was a little girl. It's not a very father/son gesture.

The drive home is silent. I eat my ice cream soup and try not to notice the fact that my dad is sniffling. When he parks the car, he turns to me, eyes red and full. "I'm trying, all right?"

"It was great, Dad. Thanks."

"You're welcome." He gets out of the car, slamming the door and hurrying inside.

"And thanks for the ice cream." I barely hear "Any time" in return because he's already upstairs.

Pete is watching TV, of course. His latest fix is *Survivorman*, which is a pretty cool show because it's easy to remember how good you have it after you've watched the guy in the Amazon or Antarctica for a week. It makes me grateful for hot water and toilet paper.

I plop down next to him on the couch. "Can we switch it to VH1?"

Pete throws me the remote. "I've already seen this one."

I change it to VH1 Classic and we watch a Michael Jackson video retrospective. It's close to the anniversary of when he died, so of course everyone wants to talk about how wonderful he was. He's still not Elvis.

Pete is inspired, so he gets up and starts working on his moonwalk, and I start trying to do the circle slide, and we end up laughing so hard my mom comes down to find out what's going on.

"Would you two please be quiet?" She's not upset, but she's not necessarily amused, either.

"Sorry," Pete says.

"Sorry, Mom." I whisper it, so she knows we'll tone it down.

"Stop having so much fun, all right?" She smiles her mom smile at us, the one that says we're forgiven.

"See you in the morning." I hug her, a little too hard because I almost knock her over.

She's so surprised she laughs. "Good night, kids." She leaves, and Pete and I settle in with another episode of *Survivorman*.

If anybody tries to hurt my family, I'll strangle them with my bare hands.

THE UGLY CHILDREN BRIGADE IS THE NEW ELVIS BECAUSE THEY'RE COOLER THAN COOL

Friday night. The Vibe show is locked in, nailed down, tight as it can get. Tonight we hang out at the B side wall. It's seventy-two hours until Summer Mondays in the Cities. I haven't been able to eat since this morning.

I have on my dusky plum shirt but with some cargo shorts and Tevas. Paige matched me before we came down to the station, and now she's standing next to me, watching all the meters on the board. I see her hand sneak out towards a volume slider.

"Don't touch a single thing."

She jumps back. "I'm not."

"But you were thinking about it."

The awkwardness between us seems to be gone, which is fine, because I'd rather be a BFF than a perpetual stress

217

ball. There will be other girls. Just no one like her. It's crossed my mind to text Heather, but I haven't. Not yet.

John's sitting in the corner, fiddling with a cigarette and flipping my Zippo open and closed. "It was so much nicer when we could smoke on the air."

"Yeah, but it's much healthier not to smoke at all. And would you quit fiddling with that thing?"

He chuckles. "Don't be surly. The Vibe show is perfect. You've rehearsed and fiddled with it forever. And you could do a Beautiful Music show in your sleep, so everything's just right. You're perfect on both counts." He glances at the clock. "And you're on in three seconds."

"Welcome, welcome, to Beautiful Music for Ugly Children right here on community radio, 90.3, KZUK. I'm Gabe, your host, and tonight is a tribute show—to radio. You heard me right—radio, in all its craziness. Where would I be without radio? Nowhere. To start us off, let's hear one of the masters himself, Elvis Costello, along with the Attractions, with 'Radio, Radio.'" The song unleashes itself on the airwaves with unmistakable enthusiasm.

John's beaming. "Nothing like unbridled youth to wake people up. So what's up tonight after Elvis C?"

"LL Cool J, Flo Rida, Queen, R.E.M., Chuck Brodsky, George Jones, Joni Mitchell, Regina Spektor, Donna Summer, Rancid, Tom Petty & the Heartbreakers, ZZ Top, and Wall of Voodoo. In that order."

He nods. "And the ones for your Vibe show?"

Like I don't know. He's just testing me. "Elvis Costello, Rancid, Flo Rida, ZZ Top, and Wall of Voodoo."

"And your secret song?" We've thought about a million different ones, and I finally came up with my final choice last night. It'll bring the house down.

"You won't know until I play it," I tell him. John and Paige are coming with me.

"Perfect." He gestures to the door. "I'm going outside."

Paige takes over John's chair. "Did you really bring Donna Summer?" She hates disco.

"'On the Radio' was an obvious choice."

Elvis Costello slides into LL Cool J, then he's over and I'm back on. "Who would have guessed, Ugly Children, that more than a hundred years ago, someone would invent something as marvelous as a radio? It's hard not to love an object that brings you the wonderfulness of music, even music like Flo Rida's. I have no idea if airplay matters to a musician's career today, but it might. You never know. Let's roll a little funky with his song 'Radio,' on 90.3, KZUK."

It sounds like a Top 40 station in here. Gross.

John comes back into the studio after Queen. He gives me the thumbs-up as I talk, then motions Paige to get back out of the chair he'd been sitting in. She does, but she gives him a look, which he doesn't see.

"Tonight, Ugly Children, what would you like to do? How about another go at B side graffiti? Name it, claim it, write it all over, and let's let R.E.M. accompany you. Their A sides are as cool as their B sides. Here's 'Radio Free Europe,' some old-school alt rock on KZUK, 90.3 community radio."

Paige groans. "You just think you're as cool as a B side."

"I'm cooler than your B side, that's for sure." I tug her hair, which is quite lovely tonight, but I don't mention it. "How about if we put your B side and my B side together and make some beautiful music?" My smile tips Paige into anger, and she storms out of the studio.

John watches her go. "She's a bit sensitive, isn't she?"

"Well, we had a … moment … a while ago, and she's not sure what to think about it."

"You mean like a moment-moment?"

"Not quite like that, but we … kissed. More to prove a point to Mara, but we kissed."

"Hot damn! I told you it would be all right." He claps me on the shoulder.

I frown. "Having her best friend turn into her boy-friend isn't her thing."

"Too bad. Guess there's not much you can do about it." He points at the CD player. "But you've got more pressing matters—like dead air."

"Pardon me, fans, listen to the big old pause. Chalk it up to live clowns in the studio. Time now for some Chuck Brodsky, and his song called 'Radio.' I know, I know, repetitive titles. But enjoy it anyway."

Once I'm done, I tell John to steer the ship while I go find Paige. Not like she's disappeared—she's gone no farther than the back door, and she's smoking a cigarette, something she never does.

"Where'd you get that?" I pull it out of her fingers and put it out.

"John left his pack down here." She shows me his Marlboros and my Zippo. "You really need to watch your mouth."

"Can I help it?" I try to keep it light. "I wanted that kiss to mean something, and you shot me down."

She's turned away from me, lighting another one. "I didn't shoot you down. I just told you it's not possible."

"Why not?" I grab my Zippo back from her. "It could work."

"Yeah, well … boyfriends are easy to find. Best friends … not so much." Her eyes are soft, even if her words are trying to be hard, and she's close to tears. Paige does not get close to tears.

Even though I don't want to, I hear her. Then I hold out my hand. "Would you please come inside?"

She stubs out her butt and puts it in the ashtray, then takes my hand.

John's excited when we get back to the studio. "I talked to the UCB! I told them to get ready for your visit, and that you couldn't wait to meet them, and then I played Conway Twitty." He's quite pleased with himself.

"You have your own show, dude."

"Yeah, but it's the UCB! And there was no dead air— did I ever tell you my best no-dead-air story?" He settles into the legend. "It was Halloween, 1962 or so, and I was on the second floor of a building in San Diego, watching the crowd downtown have a huge outdoor Halloween party. They were watching me, too."

"Did you have a costume?" Paige wants the details.

He gives her a look. "Just a mask. But that doesn't matter."

He sails on. "There was a balcony on our floor, and I went out to get some candy and wave at folks, and I locked myself out. Can you believe that? Here I was, pockets full of Halloween candy and a minute left on my song, and no way to get back to the studio!"

"Did you have to call someone?" I can picture John eating Halloween candy and waving to people in the street below, then cursing his head off when he realizes the door is locked.

"Nope. I jumped off the balcony, scraped my hands when I landed, twisted my ankle, lost all my Halloween candy, tore open a window with my bare hands, which made them even more bloody, then climbed in the building and ripped two doors off their hinges to get inside the studio. With no dead air. I even had enough breath to talk before I put on the next record."

"Which was?" I know he'll know.

"'Searchin',' by the Coasters. Pretty good story, huh? That's me, ol' Super DJ."

Paige doesn't quite believe him, but I do. While she grills him about the heroic leap off the balcony, I give the UCB more songs to dance to. Then we get to the final cuts. "All right, listeners, you're full of radio songs now. Let's close out our night with two more bursts of energy, both of them dedicated to the old-school humongous-ass AM stations in Mexico. Here's 'Heard it on the X' from ZZ Top, and 'Mexican Radio' from Wall of Voodoo. See you next week, listeners. This is Gabe, signing off of Beautiful Music for Ugly Children, right here on community radio 90.3, KZUK. I'm off to claim my B side."

Even though they're not quite my flavor, ZZ Top makes me smile. Nothing like Texas rock at one a.m.

John's shoving CDs in their cases and gathering everything into the crate. "UCB, here we come!"

Paige turns to me. "Ready to meet your fan club?"

"Not really." My stomach feels like I've swallowed my pepper spray.

"They'll love you because you look so good. Who's your personal shopper?" It's the first smile I've seen out of her all night.

"Her name is Paige, and she's really good. Just don't kiss her."

"What's this I hear about kissing?" John's shutting lights off while making sure Marijane is gardening her butt off. He elbows me in the side, and Paige sees him.

"NOBODY. SAID. ANYTHING. ABOUT. KISS-ING." Each pause is punctuated by a whack over the head with Paige's handbag, which is big enough to hide a small child in, and that must be what she has in there because it's heavy and it hurts.

We pile in John's Caddy. Paige is in the back seat, and I hope she doesn't decide to hit me again with whatever's in that bag. John tells us more about his radio days. Jumping off a balcony and locking himself out for Halloween candy is one of the less stupid things he did.

"Do you know where you're going? You're two streets

west of where you need to be." Paige sounds like a diva actress directing her driver somewhere.

"Sorry." John's turning corners, getting back to where we need to be. "I thought they were expecting him at 1:30."

"That may be, but he still can't be late."

It's only 1:15, and I hadn't even noticed we were on the wrong street because I'm too busy trying to figure out what to do if they all laugh at me.

Suddenly we're there. I close my eyes and ask the universe for fifteen seconds of goodness. Just fifteen seconds.

When I open my eyes, I see a crowd by the graffiti wall. Maybe twenty people. Not sixty-eight, but not ten.

My legs are shaking. I don't know if I can do this.

John parks, hops out, and opens my door before I get my brain together. "Presenting … Gabe!"

They could throw eggs, or cold spaghetti, or rocks.

But one person starts to clap. Then another. Then they're all clapping, long and loud, like it's 1954 and I'm Elvis. John and Paige are whistling and cheering right along with them. The only thing I can think to do is bow, so I do.

These people like Gabe. Me.

Then everyone stops looking and starts chatting again. People are coming over. A guy hands me a cup full of something that smells like Hawaiian Punch with a distinct alcohol edge. "Don't drink it too fast. It's pretty strong." He walks off while another girl points me toward a bunch of chip bags, Subway sandwich wrappers, and Oreo cookie packages laid out on top of a car hood. "If you're hungry."

Then someone grabs me, and it's Bobby X. "You're

crazy good. How do you find all that shit?" He's more animated than I've ever seen him.

I nod toward John. "My neighbor is a DJ too."

Bobby X actually shakes my hand. "You're awesome, Liz. Gabe." And he wanders off.

Then Marci Anderson comes up to me. We've been in at least one class together every semester since ninth grade. "Why didn't you ever tell anybody about Gabe? He's really interesting!" Then she blushes. "I mean, you. You're really interesting. Sorry."

"It's not the easiest thing to tell someone."

She blushes again. "Your show's great." She scurries away.

After that, nobody calls me Liz. I chat with people, and sometimes I hear myself laughing. Like honest-to-god laughing, because people are saying funny things, and I feel comfortable, so I laugh. It feels so good. Liz never laughed.

Paige, of course, is in her element, flirting with everyone. John's having a good time, too, chatting and laughing and eating chips like they'll disappear out of stores tomorrow. Nobody minds talking to him, because he's doing his best to be his charming DJ self. I wonder if he introduced himself when he was on the air.

I scan the crowd—no Heather. That's probably good. I see Mara standing over by the car-hood table, and she's by herself so I decide to talk to her. I've been thinking about this for a while.

She's grabbing some Oreos, so I reach over her hand to snag one. "I'm surprised to see you here."

"Oh! Hi, uh … hi, Gabe." I can see her cheeks get red, even under the streetlight. "Um … how are you?"

"Really fine, actually. I need to thank you."

"For what?" It's obvious this isn't what she was expecting to come out of my mouth.

"For outing me. You shoved me off the cliff. Turns out I can fly." God, that's dorky. But it's what it feels like.

"Oh. Well. I guess you're welcome." She walks away with her handful of Oreos and a backward glance over her shoulder. I can tell she thinks I've lost it. I probably have.

All of a sudden I hear a voice yell, "Get the hell out of here!" from somewhere behind me. Then I'm shoved in the shoulder and a different voice says in my ear, "What a waste of humanity!"

When I whirl around, I realize the voice in my ear is Scream, who's standing behind me. Jason is walking toward me from the outside of the circle, baseball bat in hand. The crowd noise starts to die as people see the two of them, looking out of place and creepy in their masks.

"Stop it, guys. If you leave, there won't be trouble." This voice belongs to a guy I don't know. He's walking towards me and Scream, arms out in a *let's keep the peace* gesture. "Please just go."

Jason stops the guy with a raised hand. "We're just here to talk."

"With a baseball bat? Just go and nobody gets hurt." Keep the Peace Guy is serious. Nobody else in the crowd has moved a muscle.

"We want a word with It, all right? We've told her for

226

a long time we'd be coming to find her." Scream reaches out and grabs my elbow, but his hand is instantly removed.

"You've got no business here." It's John. "I'm calling the cops if you don't leave now."

"Listen here, old fart, it's obvious you think It's precious." Jason just can't shut up. "We, on the other hand, want to help It."

"Go crash someone else's party." John doesn't want to fight, but he will, in an instant. I can see it in his face.

"You shouldn't post your party times on public places like Facebook."

I look to see where Paige is, and she's next to the car-hood table. She's safe there. Her eyes are enormous.

I point at Jason. "Thought you were coming to my house last week. We had Popsicles for you."

Scream grabs my arm again and tries to pull me to him. "Fucking gender-bender dipshit. Get your ass over here."

I try to rip my arm back from him. "Take off your masks, chickenshits. When you attack a man, do it with your real face."

Jason throws his mask on the ground and it's Paul Willard. "You stole my girlfriend, asshole. And you lied to us."

I start to laugh. "Everybody standing here knows who I am. There's no lying going on. And losing your girlfriend's not my fault. You have to read her texts to find out she's not that into you?"

"Shut up!"

"Or are you pissed she wanted a guy like me?"

Paul's in front of me now, and I can see the effect of

227

those words. He shoves me in the chest with the end of the bat, hard enough that my body slams into John, who's right behind me. "Ever see *American History X*? Skinhead slams a black kid's head on a curb."

Scream grabs my hair. "Your turn. Right here. Right now."

Keep the Peace Guy yells and starts toward me. "Let go of him!"

John's pulling me away from Scream. Then I hear the bat connect.

And John goes down.

Hands restrain me, holding me back from killing Paul and Scream. At some point I realize I'm yelling but I'm not saying any words. Once the crowd clears, I can see that Paul's on the ground. The baseball bat is next to him. Keep the Peace Guy has his foot on Paul's throat, and there's blood on his hands and Paul's face.

The Scream mask is next to Paul on the ground, and next to the Scream mask is Kyle Marshall. Nobody's got a foot on Kyle because he's out cold.

Paige is kneeling beside John. Someone's turned him over so he's on his back. I break away from whoever's got me and stumble toward them. Once I fall next to Paige, I can see the utter stillness on John's face, like someone's sucked out his being and left his sack of bones behind. When I concentrate on his chest, I see it rise. Barely. There's no blood. Just an empty, barely breathing sack of bones.

"Has anybody called 911?" My brain's so numb that I'm making sense. "An ambulance?"

Paige can't talk because she's weeping so hard, but she nods. She strokes John's hair and I take his hand, watching his chest and how slow it's moving. Nobody says a word, though I can tell people are shifting around us. But it's my job to watch John's chest. If I lose my focus, it won't go up and down anymore.

Finally, finally, finally the ambulance roars up. They put John's stillness on the gurney and sweep him away, lights blazing and sirens crying.

Then the cop cars show up, making just as much noise as the ambulance, and Keep the Peace Guy lets Paul off the ground so the cops can take him. Kyle is awake now, so he gets shoved in the cop car, too. I'm apologizing to everyone standing around, and they're patting me on the shoulder, it's not my fault, things will be okay, things will be just fine. All I can see in my mind's eye is John. So still.

From the back seat of the cop car, Paul yells at me. "You brought this all on yourself, fuckwad! You and your he-she-it bullshit!"

In spite of everything, I laugh. "A dude with a pussy swiped your girlfriend. How hilarious is that?"

I really must be a guy if other guys want to fight me.

An officer approaches me. "Can we talk to you ... sir?"

It's the one from when John and I went to the cop shop the first time, the one who spent the whole time sneering.

"I need to get to the hospital."

"We'll follow you there." The squad car drives away with Paul and Kyle in it, and the cop gets in the other one to wait for me.

I feel I like should say something to the crowd before I go. They're around me in a wide circle.

"I … well … the Ugly Children Brigade is over. No more radio show."

"You can't do that!" From my left.

"No way, Gabe." From my right.

"We won't quit." From behind me.

Then there are more shouts of "Don't stop now" and one "Fine, I'll be the DJ instead."

Paige waves her hands around. "Don't listen to him. He's not talking sense right now."

I head for John's Cadillac, hoping the keys are in it instead of in John's pocket, and Keep the Peace Guy meets me at the car. "I'm Jake Richmond." He sticks out his hand and I shake it. "I'm really sorry."

"Thanks for sticking up for me." I'm not sure what else to say.

"Sure."

"You don't even know me."

"So?" He looks at the blood on his hands. "Hope your grandpa's okay."

"Um … yeah. Me too." We shake hands again. Then Paige gets in the front seat while I grab the keys from the ashtray, where I thought they'd be, and we drive John's big boat of a Cadillac to the hospital, police car trailing us.

On the way, I look down and realize Paul's blood is on me, from where Jake shook my hand. Then my brain shorts out, and I start to hyperventilate. Paige makes me pull over, and then the cop comes and looks in our window.

"Can't you see he's having a panic attack?" Paige screeches at the guy.

I try and breathe normally. "Give me a second."

"Take your time, sir." The cop looks less like a smart-ass, watching me struggle to breathe, and he goes back to his car with a few glances over his shoulder.

I get it together and get back on the road to the hospital.

"Who was Paul's girlfriend?" A tiny voice from the corner of the front seat.

"Heather Graves." I keep my eyes on the road.

"She texted you?"

"Yeah."

"What the hell did those texts say if he was that mad at you?"

No way am I going to tell her.

"Fine. Don't tell me." Silence. "But she dumped a guy every other month."

"Maybe so, but nobody wants the trans man to steal their girlfriend."

She snorts. "A guy with a pussy." Then a pause. "Were you going to go out with her?"

"I turned her down." I reach out for her hand with my bloody one, and she takes it.

231

Silence. We drive.

"I hope John's all right." The tears are trickling down her face.

"Yeah." That's all I can say, or I'll lose it.

By the time we get to the hospital, John's been there for at least half an hour. The cops meet us at the front door, and we answer all the cops' questions. Yes, they threatened us in the parking lot of KZUK. Yes, we reported them a few weeks ago, and so did Frank at Video Rewind when they came back to attack Paige. Yes, they threatened my family. No, they never showed up. Yes, we'll testify in court. All I can think about is John's stillness.

When we finally get inside the emergency room, no one will tell us anything because we're not his next of kin. I can't think what else to do, so I call my parents, and they come and convince the doctors that we're the closest thing he has to family. Finally a doctor leads us into a little room. Paige comes, too, because the doctors think she's my sister. My mom's patting Paige on the back, and my dad's got his hand on my shoulder. Nobody sits down.

The doctor has a name card clipped to her scrubs that says *DR. ANDERSON*. She consults her clipboard. "Your neighbor is John Burrows?"

"Right." My dad's taken over, and I'm so glad.

"Mr. Burrows is under serious sedation while his brain swelling goes down. He took quite a blow. Do you know what he was hit with?" Dr. Anderson looks at Dad, and Dad looks at me.

"A baseball bat." I can barely say it.

"That kind of trauma will throw anyone for a loop, but given Mr. Burrows' age, he may not recover."

The words fall on the tile floor like stones.

"Ever?" My dad sounds just as shocked as I feel.

"You need to know the seriousness of his injury." Dr. Anderson reads her clipboard again. "Mr. Burrows is in good health otherwise, so he may surprise us, but some people who sustain these kinds of injuries remain in a vegetative state for the rest of their lives."

"I...I see." My dad is calm.

I am not. "For real? He might not wake up?"

Dr. Anderson looks me square in the eye. "Correct."

My whole body would scream if it could. "John will prove you wrong, I know it. He's strong. He'll come back." Paige has her arm around my shoulders, and my dad is right next to me. I'm not sure they know they're keeping me from falling down.

Flip flip flip through a few more sheets of paper. "He's in ICU for now, until we determine when we can bring him out of sedation. Room 5525. If one of you would like to visit, you're welcome to. But only for five minutes an hour." She attempts to smile. "I wish I had better news."

Dad shakes her hand. "Thanks for your time." Dr. Anderson leaves.

"We have to call Patrick and Margaret."

"Who are they?" Dad turns to me.

"His kids."

My mom is shocked, almost angry. "You know where his kids are?"

"He told me a few weeks ago. They're in Chicago and Seattle."

"Maybe they're in his phone." Paige points toward the nurse's station. "Go find it."

I ask a nurse about John's personal things, and she says they're right here, are we the next of kin? I say yes, and she gives me a white plastic bag. Inside are John's clothes, his reading glasses, and his cell phone. When I open the contacts list, there are four numbers: me, my house, Patrick, and Margaret.

I hand the bag to Mom. "Would you take this to John's house? The spare key's under the bust of Elvis on the porch." She nods.

"Do you want me to call them?" Dad holds out his hand for the phone.

"I'll do it."

He looks between me and Paige. "Are you two going to stay for a while?"

I nod at him but then look at Paige. "You can go if you want."

She shakes her head. "I'm staying with you."

"We'll see you in the morning—I guess it is morning—we'll see you when you get home." My mom hugs each of us, then follows my dad to the elevator.

I find a nurse again and ask where 5525 is. She points

down the hall. "Only one visitor for five minutes every hour." The crabby look she gives me says she means it.

In room 5525, there are two beds, and one is empty. The other one is full of a person who looks like John but is also empty. When I look down at him, there's no laughter, no jokes, no Southern accent. No music. I touch his hand, and he's cold.

It's all my fault. Me and my weirdness.

I stare at him as hard as I can, willing him to wake up, but then I remember he can't because he's in a coma so his brain will heal. The crabby nurse comes to the door, sliding her finger across her throat to tell me I'm cut off for the next 55 minutes, and I back out of the room, willing him to wake up in spite of the medication. He's that powerful. I know it.

Paige is on a bench by the nurse's station. "How does he look?"

"Like a corpse." I sit down next to her. "It's my fault."

"It's Paul and Kyle's fault."

"What if John never wakes up?"

"He will. He's strong." She leans on me, and I let her. We sit that way for a little while.

"Do you think they'd let me spend the night here?"

"I have no idea." She's moved away from me and leaned back on the wall, looking as tired as I feel. Her makeup is streaked down her face and there's blood on her skirt from where she helped Jake clean off his hands. But she is still, eternally, beautiful.

I find a nurse again, this time a very kind young one,

and she gives me a disposable toothbrush and points me down the hall to a family sleeping room with a pullout couch. I go back to Paige and tell her where I'm going. She says she'll see me tomorrow. Big hug in the hall. It's all I can do to brush my teeth, and I'm gone the instant my head hits the pillow.

At some point during the night I wake up. It takes me a second to remember where I am, and sadness sweeps across me like a thunderstorm. Then I realize there's someone in bed with me, and an arm is draped across my stomach. Then I feel something across my face, and I realize it's hair. Paige's hair.

Paige is in bed with me.

So I go back to sleep, sadness pushed aside for one peaceful, wonder-filled moment. What if it's a dream? If it is, I want it to last as long as possible.

ELVIS IS THE NEW ELVIS BECAUSE DUH, THERE'S ONLY ONE ELVIS

Saturday. I wake up at eight, and Paige is gone. Maybe I really did dream it. I'm not going to ask.

Saturday noon. John's still knocked out. A different doctor tells me they un-sedate him a little every twelve hours, to check the brain swelling, but he'll be knocked out until Monday at the earliest. Then they'll bring him out of his drug coma and see what happens. I call Paige and leave a message on her phone.

Saturday afternoon. I call John's kids. Patrick tells me his father died in 1974, how dare I bother him now, and where did I get this number? I tell him from his father's cell phone. Margaret tells me she'll be there on Sunday, and then she asks me to forgive Patrick for being rude. He'd already called her to tell her what happened.

Saturday night. Paige asks if I want her at the hospital, but I say no. It's my job to watch over him. Only me. This is my fault.

I go home to take a shower and change my clothes. Then I'm back, in John's room for five minutes every hour. At midnight the nurse kicks me out when I ask her for another disposable toothbrush.

I haven't looked at the Facebook page for the UCB. I don't even want to know.

Sunday morning.

"Are you reading that book or staring at it?"

"Staring at it." Holy crap. "Who told you I was here?"

"I guessed." Heather sits down next to me on the bench by the nurse's station. "I'm sorry."

"For what?"

"I didn't know Paul was coming after you."

"I didn't figure you did."

Nobody says anything for a while.

"Are you still interested?"

I look at the side of her face, because she's staring into the nurse's station, watching them type all their notes about who needs what pills and who's getting better. Or worse. Or not moving at all.

"I can't right now."

She sighs. "Paige is better for you, anyway."

"The jury's still out on that one."

She smiles at me. "I'd just dump you in the end."

"You don't know that." Now it's my turn to smile.

She kisses me, ever so softly, and gets up. "No, I don't." Then she's gone, around the corner of the nurse's station and down the hall.

I don't even pretend to read my book. I just stare after her.

Sunday afternoon. Margaret comes.

She's nice, but very distant. She tells the doctors she's his daughter, yes, but they've not been close for many, many years.

It's almost shocking how much she looks like John. Same features, same body shape, same laugh. I know because she laughed when I told her she looked like John. Maybe that was the wrong thing to say.

After she talks to Dr. Anderson, she finds me on my bench.

"So you're Dad's neighbor?" Her eyes are kind, but she's guarded.

"Right. His...student, I guess. He got me a radio show."

She smiles. "Radio always was his first love. How did he get hurt?"

"He was with me. Meeting my fans."

"You have fans?" This surprises her. "I don't get the connection between meeting fans and getting hurt."

"It's a long story."

"Try me." She doesn't seem mad that it's my fault.

"Well...there are people who don't like me. And they came by when I was meeting the Ugly Children Brigade and they accidentally hit your dad instead of me."

"Ugly Children Brigade? They wanted to hit you?"

"Another long story."

She considers what I've said, then looks at me like she hasn't quite seen me up to this point. "Well, I'm sure he was doing what he loves, which is talking to people and talking about music, so if he doesn't recover, at least he was happy when he got hurt." She pauses. "It's strange to see him after all this time, especially when he doesn't know I'm here. We send cards at Christmas, but that's all." She looks at me again, really looks. "His cards always mention his smart, funny neighbor who loves music. And that can only be you. I don't see anyone else visiting him every hour." She smiles. "I can come back in a couple weeks. Will you call me every day? Let me know how he is?"

"Sure. Of course."

She stands up and looks at the clock over the nurse's station. "I'm going to check on him before I go. Good thing flights between Chicago and Minneapolis are cheap." She shakes my hand. "I'm glad he has someone to see his good side."

It comes rushing out before I stop to think. "I thought you hated him."

"No." Now her smile is sad. "He might not have been the best dad, but he's always been a good guy." She turns and walks down the hall toward 5525. "Thanks again, Liz." To John, I was still Liz at Christmas time.

The grouchy nurse is behind the desk, and I see her look at the clock when Margaret enters the room. She may give Margaret three minutes if she's lucky.

Paige, Heather, Paul Willard, Margaret: people don't do what you think they're going to do. Maybe everyone has a B side, or a C side. Or an R side. Maybe all of them.

Monday noon. I call Paige. "They're un-sedating him this afternoon."

"Do you want me to be there with you?"

"Yes please." I've crumbled. I need her.

"I'll be there at 3:30."

I call Margaret, so she knows.

At 3:45, Dr. Anderson comes to talk to us at my bench. "We've discontinued the sedatives. If he's going to wake up, he'll do it in the next week."

My hand is crushing Paige's. "What if he doesn't?"

"If he doesn't wake up within a week, well … we'll have to decide what's next." She gives us a sympathetic look and heads down the hall.

Paige squeezes my hand, then lets it go. "Are you ready for tonight?"

"What the hell is tonight?"

"The Vibe?"

"That's tomorrow."

"Look." Paige points at the nurse's station. "Today's the twelfth."

"Tomorrow is the twelfth." I squint in the direction of the calendar.

"If you don't get your ass in the car, you're going to be late and blow it altogether."

"You're full of shit." I get up to go look, just to be able to prove my point.

"NO I'M NOT." Paige is yelling and pointing, and

at least three nurses have poked their heads out of patient rooms to see what's going on.

But there it is, in big red numbers on the calendar: Monday July 12.

"This isn't happening." I'm so loud a nurse tells me to shush. I need to stay. I can't go.

John would be furious if I didn't go.

I grab Paige's arm. "Can you stay here and be here with him, just in case he wakes up?"

"Can I go home and get my book?"

"I don't care, but hurry, and you have to call me every hour after your five minutes. Leave a message if I don't answer." I hug her quick.

"You're welcome. Don't forget your lucky clothes."

"Gotta stop at home and pick up my CD anyway. Call me!" And I sprint for the parking lot.

I bust my ass getting home, changing, and getting on the road. My guilt keeps me company on the drive. I shouldn't have left the hospital. I shouldn't have let him get me a show. I shouldn't have flirted with Heather. I should have stayed Liz. I should have mowed his lawn more often. I should have bought him more birthday gifts. I should have told him what he means to me.

Summer Mondays in the Cities is deep in downtown Minneapolis, of course, but the rush hour traffic is going out of town instead of coming in so the drive isn't too slow.

Paige calls twice to tell me there's no change. She was supposed to be with me. John too. They're not supposed to be in a crap-ass hospital.

The first thing I see when I get to Loring Park is a huge banner that says *SUMMER MONDAYS IN THE CITIES*, strung between light towers over a stage. There are parking spots close to the stage, and one of them has my name on a sign in front of it: *THE VIBE 89.1, GABE WILLIAMS*. It feels really strange, but cool, to have a parking space with my name on it, because otherwise I'd have to park six blocks away. When I get out, I'm met by a cute girl in the same Stones T-shirt I bought at Target, plus purple Chucks to complete her roadie outfit. She doesn't toss her hair. Instead she introduces me to Sheldon, the program director of the Vibe, and Thad, the station manager, who tells me my time, 11:30 to midnight, which fits my late-night preferences. They point at a tent where the other four contestants are waiting. Snacks and water are there, they say.

I wade through the crowd, and one guy spills his beer on me. Another woman stares. Like, stares. Then she realizes what she's doing and blushes, then whispers, "Sorry." Maybe I'm not Gabe enough, but there's no way to fix it now.

Once I make it to the tent, I grab a bottle of water and mentally go over the order of the songs on my CD—Elvis Costello, Rancid, Flo Rida, ZZ Top, and Wall of Voodoo, plus my secret weapon—and think about the scripts I've written out, over and over again, getting ready for this moment. Then I see John stretched out on the ground, still as midnight. The other contestants milling around in the tent have all brought wives or girlfriends—except for the girl contestant, who brought an old dude who looks a lot like Iggy Pop—and they try to chat me up, so I make polite conversation. If they're checking me out, they're doing it on the sly. Nobody acts like I could be anybody but someone named Gabe.

Their small talk is different than most people's. One of them knows Prince personally, and one of them used to tour with Green Day as a roadie, and did I know that Billie Joe Armstrong's wife Adrienne went to college in Maxfield? Yes, I did, but please don't talk to me, because I'm too busy thinking about my almost-dead friend while I try to remember what I'm supposed to say between ZZ Top and Wall of Voodoo.

By the time we get to eleven o'clock, the crowd is huge. Every time a new contestant's left the tent to go on, I've gone out to listen, and every time I realize I'm better than the person on stage, better a thousand times over. The crowd doesn't much care—they're there to have fun and dance. In between contestants, the Vibe plays other music, and there's a tech guy who makes the lights do funky things while each contestant is on, so the crowd likes that. But Sheldon and Thad care—they're watching closer than close.

The second contestant played Donna Summer, and someone in the crowd hollered "Disco died a million years ago!" The third contestant played LL Cool J, and someone yelled, "Boring!" I wonder what they're going to holler at me.

Since seven, Paige has called three more times to say

nothing's changed. Now my brain is full of furious and ter-rified static.

When it's finally 11:30, I step on the stage and mum-ble "Hi, I'm Gabe" into the mic. Then I proceed to suck. Suck like a fancy vacuum, in fact. My voice has no punch, and everything I say sounds hollow and dumb. People dance, but everyone used up their energy on the first four contestants. One person yells "ZZ Top! Woo!" and one person yells "Flo Rida sucks!" but that's about it. It's late, it's almost Tuesday, and people have to work tomorrow.

When I put on my secret song, which is "Soul Fin-ger" by the Bar-Kays, made famous again by its inclusion on the *Superbad* soundtrack, the crowd perks up. They all shout "soul finger!" every time it comes up in the song while they groove around in front of the stage. It's the only time I feel sort of normal.

I can do this: on the air, in a park, wherever. But music's about emotion, and I can't scream "soul finger" when my heart feels dead.

When I'm done, my stomach hurts because I was so horrible. I know I've pissed the guest spot down my leg when Sheldon shakes my hand and says "Beautiful Music for Ugly Children is really pretty good, but that was ... well, we'd expected more from you." Thad smiles like someone's died, and it's possible someone has, but I don't say that. I shake their hands, tell them I'm sorry, and get in my car after I've swiped the *THE VIBE 89.1, GABE WILLIAMS* sign from the parking spot. I'll put it in my scrapbook.

By the time I'm halfway home, I can't do it anymore. I

246

pull over and let the tears destroy me. Half an hour later, I can finally see again.

When I get back to the hospital, it's three a.m. Paige is asleep on my bench, phone in her hand. When I shake her shoulder, she starts. "You dumbshit! Why haven't you answered your phone?"

"My phone hasn't rung."

"Yes it has! Look at it!"

When I check it, there are three missed calls and five texts. I'd put it on silent right before I went on the air and forgot to change it. I call my voicemail.

Paige swats my phone away from my ear. "I'm right here, fool. He woke up!"

"He did?"

"He asked for you."

My brain's on fire. "Were you there? He asked for me?"

"How the hell do you think I know he woke up? I went in for my five minutes and was talking to him about your Vibe show, that it was tonight, and he opened his eyes and mumbled 'Where's Gabe?' At least that's what I thought he said. Then he passed out."

I'm crying again. "How long until we can go in?"

She checks the clock. "Ten minutes. How did it go, by the way?"

"John in his coma could have done better."

"No way." She pats my back until I stop crying. Then

it's time for me to go into his room. When I creep up to his bed, his eyes are shut.

"John?"

No movement, no eye flickers.

I tell him how bad I was at the Vibe, just so he knows, and I talk to him about what I'm planning for Friday, which is complete bullshit, because I have no idea what I'm planning for Friday. Still no response.

When my five minutes are up, I go back out to Paige. "You must have imagined it."

"I promise you, I heard it." She can see I'm almost in tears again. "You realize all this weeping isn't very manly."

I know she's trying to lighten the moment, but it's not the right thing to say.

"If he woke up once, he'll do it again." She's got her hand on my knee. "You know I'm just joking about the crying."

"Not a single thing in the universe is funny right now."

She jumps up and stands in front of me like a drill sergeant, hands on her hips. "I've got something. You'll be in hysterics."

"Let me guess—you're really a man. And was that you in bed with me the other night?"

"I'm not a man, and yes it was. Get over it." She frowns. "In the interest of making you laugh, I'm gonna show you something."

Paige puts her hand down her shirt and does something, then pulls it back out and opens her fingers very slowly. In her palm is a piece of flannel, white and maybe two inches square.

I lean a little bit off the bench so I can see. "What is it?"

"Part of my wubbie."

"Your wubbie?"

"Do you remember, when we were in kindergarten, I sometimes brought my wubbie to school?"

In my mind I see a girl with a pink blanket over her shoulder. "Your baby blanket is your secret?"

"The secret is that I wear it in my bra every day. On the left side, close to my heart."

It works. I laugh. "Why do you need your baby blanket close to your heart?"

"It makes me feel safe."

"Like my Mango. Shall I show it to you?" I start to unzip. Her mouth is hanging wide open.

"I know you want to see it again."

"Not now!" Paige recovers and tucks the flannel back into her bra. "So what if my big secret isn't as big as yours. It's big to me." I think I might have hurt her feelings.

"I will keep it close to my own heart. I promise."

She comes back to the bench and I pick up her hand and hold it. Then Paige clears her throat. "I have one more secret."

"What's that?" Nothing could surprise me.

"I wear butt-lifter jeans."

Except that. I laugh so hard I fall off the bench. When I recover myself enough to talk, I realize Paige has stood up. "That'll teach you to read *Vogue*, won't it? They probably have the same thing for men, and you might want them someday." Paige walks off. "I'm going to the bathroom."

"Can I come with you?"

She gives me the finger. "Not your kind of bathroom anymore."

"But I'm your BFF! And your boy FF, too!" Three nurses look up from the desk and give me three separate glares.

At least Paige doesn't contradict me.

When the next five minutes comes up, nothing's changed. It's 4:30 on Tuesday morning. We go home to get some sleep.

Tuesday afternoon. They move him to a regular room, since he seems to be out of danger. Dr. Anderson tells us it's a waiting game from now on, so I pull a chair next to John's bed and wait. What else do I have to do? I call Margaret to tell her I'm waiting. I've called her every day, like she asked.

The rest of Tuesday goes by. Chris tells me I can take time off, all I need.

Then it's Wednesday. Then it's Thursday.

Friday morning. I'm finally brave enough to check the UCB's Facebook page before I go to the hospital.

There's a photo of a big black banner that says *HATE SUCKS*, and the banner is draped on the B side wall. Then there's a photo of John at the party and the caption reads, *Get well, Mr. Guy We Think Is Named John.* Then there's a photo of me, laughing at something before Paul and Kyle crashed the party, and the caption says, *We still love you, Gabe.*

I leave a post: Thanks, you guys. I'll tell you more about John on the air. Talk to you tonight.

No change at the hospital. Margaret thanks me for keeping in touch.

Friday night. I've decided on a Beatles show, in honor of John's claim that they changed the entire world. I'm sitting by the side of his bed, chatting on about what I plan to play and how I broke into his house to swipe a few Beatles albums I don't have, and a nurse sticks her head in.

"I need to give him a sponge bath, so you'll have to step outside for a while."

"He ... stay." Barely a whisper from the bed.

I look at the nurse. "Did you hear that?" I jump up to get closer to John. "Did I imagine it?"

His eyes aren't open, but he smiles. "No."

"Oh my fucking hell, John, it's about time you came back to us." I burst into tears.

He opens his eyes a tiny slit. "Been here ... all along. Your show ... not suck."

251

"Oh yes it did! You have no idea."

"Don't … cry." He smiles again, but it's weak.

"I'm so sorry. I can't even tell you how sorry."

"… Okay … it's … okay."

"It can't be okay!"

He takes a couple breaths. "Not … your fault."

The nurse is watching us. She's new, so she doesn't know me yet. "Is this your grandpa, young man?"

"Close enough." John tries to smile again, but he's already drifting.

The nurse sets up for the sponge bath, and I decide to leave because I have no desire to see old-man flesh, even if it's this old man. Before I go, I lean close to John. "Tonight's show is for you."

"Okay." The smile flickers in again.

"I'll be back tomorrow."

"Okay."

If I could turn cartwheels all the way to the car, I would. I call Paige on my way to the station. "John woke up."

"You knew he would."

"No I didn't."

"Don't cry, silly boy."

"These are happy tears." I've cried more in the last week than I have in my entire life.

I make a quick detour back to John's house and swipe the key. In the corner of the farthest music room, there's a box with the label *OUR FAVORITES*. I grab it and run back to the car.

"Welcome, friends and neighbors, to Beautiful Music for Ugly Children. I'm Gabe, your most unusual host, as you know, and today's show is for John, my musical mentor. These songs are our favorites, so get prepared for some zany sounds. Let's start the show with a Rolling Stones track, and I want you to turn it up really loud in his honor. Every song's better when it's loud, but this one needs top volume. Here's 'Gimme Shelter,' right here on 90.3, KZUK. It's beautiful music just for you, Ugly Children."

I put the earphones on and slide the volume up as high as I can take it. Get well soon, friend.

Then it's time for more chat. "So, Ugly Children, how's your night? Hope you're hanging at the B side wall, having some chips and contemplating the world. As we know, last week's lovely get-together was rudely interrupted, and I'm sorry about that. I understand those asshats are being charged with first-degree assault, whoops, 'asshat' is a probably a FCC violation, but so what. And before I explain about John, the man who was with me, here's another song in his honor. Let's check out the Beatles and 'All You Need Is Love.'"

Maybe love brought John back to life.

When the song's over, I'm on. "All right, UCB, here's who John is. First, you need to know he's alive, though he's been in a coma, which isn't good. I don't think he'll die, but nobody really knows." My heart does a little jump at hearing the words out loud, but I keep going. "He woke up tonight and talked to me, so that's a good sign. Second, he's my neighbor. He moved in next door when I was ten, so I've known him a while. And that leads me to my action request for the night: could you please decorate his house and lawn? 1845 Roosevelt Avenue. Be Minnesota nice, okay? No stealing, and nothing gaudy or gross, just get-well wishes, something I can take pictures of. We both thank you. And third, John's my mentor. He's a DJ from way back, the first man to play Elvis on the air if you can believe it. I know I told you that fact a long time ago, but it bears repeating because it's so amazing. He knows more about music than any other soul on the planet, so you can see why I like him so much."

I can hear Elvis whispering in my brain: *See? It's really, truly all right.*

I have to breathe deeply to keep going, because the tears are there. "Fourth, he's my family. John loves me for who I am, and that's a rare thing. He landed in the hospital because of me, and he seems okay with it. I'm not, but he is, and I love him for it."

I'm biting my lip in half trying not to cry. "How about some really lovely pop music? Here's '1, 2, 3, 4' from the Plain White Ts, on community radio 90.3, KZUK. It's a little mushy, which I'm generally not, and I know it's about a romantic relationship, but listen close—the words could apply to anyone. So this one's for you, John, and you too,

Paige, because I love you as much as I love him. Thanks for saving my ass, you guys. And thank you, Ugly Children Brigade, for accepting me. I can never tell you how much that means."

The song spills into the dark air. Nothing wrong with pop-y sunshine music, even in the middle of the night.

He's gonna get better.

Thank you, Universe.

Thank you so much.

GABE WILLIAMS IS THE NEW ELVIS BECAUSE ... WHY NOT?

Mid-August.

I go next door and knock the knock we agreed on, then let myself in. John's not so fast with his cane, so answering the door is a problem, but he's smiling in the chair when I come in.

"What's new today, my friend? You look a little like the cat who swallowed a bird."

"I've got a surprise." I drag the footstool next to his chair.

Two weeks ago I had a surprise, too: an email from the Vibe saying I was their fourth choice. Not quite the suckiest, but close enough. The dude who won was the guy who knows Prince.

I felt like someone had kicked me in the gut. I didn't leave my room except to pee. I knew I'd sucked, but I

256

wanted it so bad. After twenty-four hours, John came over and climbed the stairs. It took him half an hour, but he did it, cane and all. Once I cussed him out for climbing the stairs, I told him I wouldn't listen to him, even though I knew I had to since he worked so hard to get to my room. He told me he was sorry, and it was sad, but I couldn't let the bastards get me down. I was still me, and I'd waited eighteen years to be myself, and the Vibe wasn't going to take that away from me.

After his lecture, it took him another half hour to get back downstairs. I thought about it for another three hours, but I knew he was right. And I was hungry, so I came out.

John frowns. "I remember that last surprise. You were better than him, I know it, and I bet Prince pulled some strings. This surprise is better?"

"Yup."

"I'm gonna guess, so don't tell me." He still looks rickety—he lost thirty pounds while he was in the hospital, plus his coordination's way off and his right arm is almost useless—but the spark's in his eye, and that's what matters. Now that he's not leaving the house except for his radio show, his pastime is to surf the Net and look for vintage 45s and one-hit wonders.

He grins. "You found a long-lost original pressing of 'Hot Pants.'"

"Nope. Guess again."

"You and Paige are having a baby."

"I'm not even sure how to answer that."

He chuckles. "I'm out of guesses."

"I'm going to the community college this fall. Orientation is tomorrow."

John sighs. "Well, it's not a guest spot on a cool radio station, but it's a step toward the future. Bring me the computer, will you?"

I go to the music room and get the laptop. John flips the screen up slowly, taking his time so he doesn't drop it. "Check it out. I think they put it up today." Then he turns the screen to me.

There's a new sign on the B side wall. *TIME FOR COLLEGE*, it says. *GABE, DON'T GO!*

John looks at me. "They'll be happy you're staying in town."

They won't be as happy as my mom, who will tap dance when she finds out. My parents finally figured out that college wasn't happening—no mail, no forms, no packing, no buying little fridges—and they flipped out when I told them about the Vibe show, especially after I told them I was moving anyway, to find a job and save money. They said they were used to Gabe and weren't ready to see him go, so what about the community college? They looked so sad I had to give it a shot.

"When is Margaret coming back?"

"Next week." John smiles. "Who knew a bat to the head could be a good thing? When is Paige leaving?"

"Next week."

"Sad about that?"

"Yup."

My phone vibrates.

Be there in 10.

Speak of the devil. We're going shopping for crap for her dorm room. Boring, but I'll take what I can get. Six days and she's gone.

He sighs. "Wish I'd gone to college."

"You can come with me. I saw an old guy there when I got my registration info."

"Who you calling old, sonny boy?" His eyes twinkle again.

"You, old man."

"Help me outside. I need to get some air." He shakes his cane at me.

"You got it." We get him out of the chair, and he shuffles to the door. Once he gets there, he steps slowly over the doorjamb, then leans heavy on his cane to go the rest of the way.

Once he's outside and settled into his new chair on the porch, he waves me back inside. "Go turn on some music." I find us the recording of Elvis's 1968 comeback show and put the speakers close to the windows. Then I grab us some Pepsis and head out to join him.

"It's an Elvis kind of day." He takes the can from me. "Did you tell your mom what you're doing?"

"Nobody's home. And I wanted to tell you first."

"When are you gonna legally be Gabe?" He takes a swig of Pepsi. "Isn't that important for something like a degree?"

"I've got a semester to get all the name stuff straightened

out." Community colleges will take anyone, thank god, even a guy with a girl's first name.

"Here's to the future and the Department of Vital Statistics." He holds out his can, and I clink it with mine, then we drink. "Go see what's on the kitchen table."

"What is it?"

"Another surprise."

I go back inside and find an envelope on the table, with my old name on the front of it.

John calls from the porch. "Bring it out here before you open it."

So I go back out and sit down and open my envelope. Inside is a cashier's check from a bank, made out to Elizabeth Williams, for twenty-five thousand dollars.

I drop it.

"Pick it up! Don't let the wind catch it!" John's hollering, so I grab it quick. But I can't talk.

"Better than the Vibe surprise, huh? I made it to your legal name so you could cash it now. Sorry about that."

I can barely get the words out. "Where did this come from?"

"It's part of the Tupelo guitar. The hospital wants to bleed me dry, so I had Margaret send it to New York for auction. I really wanted to save it all for you." He genuinely looks sorry, like a twenty-five thousand dollar check isn't enough.

"This isn't real."

"Now you've got whatever you need."

I've cried more in the last month than I ever want to cry again.

John touches my knee. "It's all right, son. It's gonna be all right." He pats me and whispers it until there are no more tears.

Eventually I wipe my nose on my sleeve. "What if you need more money for bills?"

"I've got a little insurance, so that helps, and there's plenty left after your check. Maybe even enough for a vacation with a lady friend. When I can use this arm better, that is." He picks up his right arm with his left and shakes it at me, like he's trying to get it to wave at me.

Another surprise. "Lady friend?" I've seen a car over here lately, but I haven't wanted to ask.

His grin tells me it's none of my business. "It's not Cher. That's all I'm saying right now. But I'll bring her to Sunday supper at some point." After he chugs more Pepsi, he looks around. "Those Ugly Children sure did a number on my house."

Even a month later, there are still streamers all over the porch, and the *GET WELL SOON* sign is still planted in the yard where they pounded it in. I have to mow around it because John won't let me take it out. The Elvis bust now has marker lipstick and a curly wig on, thanks to them, but they also brought John the cushy deck chair he's sitting in, complete with a sign pinned to it: *SIT HERE TO LISTEN TO MUSIC.* They even put a banner on my house: *WE HOPE YOU LIVE ON THIS SIDE OF JOHN. THANKS*

261

FOR BEING YOU. My dad made me take it down, but I hung it up in my room.

"So what's up for this week's show?" He takes the last swig of his Pepsi.

"All Devo, all hour."

"The Ugly Children will divorce you if you do that. How about an all Barry Manilow show?"

"I'll divorce myself if I do that."

He grins. "If you want to fight, let's scuffle about something important. Which band name is better—Mott the Hoople or Fountains of Wayne?"

And we argue and laugh until my mom comes home.

A Note from the Author

Dear Reader:

It's 2017. Five years after its publication, *Beautiful Music* is still out and about in the world, still giving people a glimpse into the life of a trans kid. I'm proud Gabe's got some staying power, but my thoughts about his book have changed.

To reiterate, I'm not an expert here—only individuals who are transgender are experts. Please also remember there are MANY voices having conversations within, about, and with the transgender community. This note will reflect some of them, but not all of them.

What's great about 2017: transgender folks are more visible now than ever before. Society has a better understanding of what a transgender identity is. Folks are more open in expressing many variations of transgender, genderqueer, gender nonconforming, gender creative, and gender flexible identities. We have a better idea of how to help folks transition earlier and better, if that's what they choose. Things aren't perfect, by any means—the horrible, hateful bathroom bills in several states demonstrate that fact—but visibility, combined with continued education and scientific discoveries, help reinforce the fact that being trans is a natural part of human variation. It's just as natural as blue eyes or brown hair. It's not a mistake, and it's not a birth defect.

Here's the big thing I want to say. Am I proud of this book? Sure. I feel like it's well-researched and well-articulated. It's done good things in the world.

Would I write this book again?

Absolutely not.

Writers are free to create characters outside of their personal identities. It's part of what we do and part of what helps us grow. But when it comes to communities that are marginalized, *voices from that community need to be prioritized over fictional voices.* Every time, all the time.

My hope is that when you put this book down, you go read an author who's transgender or genderqueer. Someone who knows Gabe's struggle for real. I can get close, but there's absolutely no way I can truly "get it." Go read a book written by someone who completely understands Gabe's life. Their voice should be your priority.

If you'd like a little primer about sex, gender, and other elements of transgender identity, read on. If not, skip to the end of this note.

***

By now, you obviously know Gabe is a trans guy. Gabe probably wouldn't be referred to as "transsexual," though he (and the medical community) still used that word in the early 2010s, when I finished the book. Gabe was assigned female at birth because he has a vagina. However, Gabe has a strong need to take testosterone and have surgery to alter his body so he's more comfortable. Not all transgender folks have that need. Please know doctors have been helping individuals match their brains and bodies up since the early-middle part of the twentieth century, but the world has contained transgender individuals since human beings came into existence.

In our world and the world of the doctors Gabe will see someday, the word "sex" indicates internal and external sexual organs as well as chromosomes. The words that fit the binary human sexes are "male" and "female," though some folks are also intersex; they have a combination of male and female primary and secondary sex characteristics. The word "gender" refers to what our brains tell us—how we understand who we are—and it covers how we see ourselves related to the socially constructed categories of "man" and "woman."

Gender and sex are not interchangeable. We are born with bodies that indicate to doctors what our chromosomes have created (our sex). In my case, the doctor looked at my genitals at birth and said, "yup, she's a girl." Turns out my brain agreed, and that makes me cisgender ("cis" means "on the same side"). However, our society made up the rest of what it means to be a "woman" (my gender). "Man" and "woman" are categories our cultures made up, and what men and women do in the world is culturally defined, not biologically determined. You know the assumptions that men go to work and women stay home with the kids, or men should fix cars and women shouldn't? We created those ideas. Making things even more complex is the fact that we can present our gender in various ways—from the clothes we wear to the pronouns we choose. Even though our culture tells us gender presentation has pretty strict rules (boys can't wear skirts or makeup!), those ideas are also just constructions.

Sexual orientation is separate from both gender and sex. You probably already know this, but sexual orientation has to do with who makes your heart go pitter-pat. A person can be gay, straight, bisexual, pansexual, asexual, queer, or somewhere in between all those possibilities. Our gender and our genitals interact with our sexual orientation, of course, but they don't determine it.

Some individuals who are transgender may choose medical intervention to feel more comfortable and aligned. Individuals who were assigned female at birth may have oophorectomies (ovary removal) and hysterectomies (uterus removal) as well as mastectomies (breast removal) when they transition. Some may opt for a phalloplasty (creation of a penis from skin grafted from other parts of their body, including an extension of the urethra). Individuals who were assigned male at birth and are transitioning may have orchiectomies (testes removal) and vaginoplasties (converting their penis into a version of a vagina). They may also have other surgeries (on their face or Adam's apple, for example) or procedures like full-body hair removal. Individuals who medically transition often take estrogen or testosterone, depending on the direction of their transition, and the hormones work both large and subtle changes on their bodies.

Some individuals who are in transition don't choose surgery, or only choose one or two procedures from a menu of many, because they don't desire surgery or they can't afford it—the surgeries aren't usually covered by insurance, and they are very expensive. But individuals who do choose medical transition almost always choose hormones.

Intersex individuals have been treated in very negative ways by the medical community. Sometimes doctors alter a baby born with intersex genitals (internal, external, or both) to make that baby identifiably male or female before the child is old enough to express a gender. When that happens, the gender of a baby's brain might not fit the genitals a doctor chose for them, and the child can grow up with a brain and body that don't match. Ideally, parents wait to alter both internal and external sex organs until the child expresses a gender and/or an opinion about what genitals seem right for them. Then the doctors perform surgery to help the child's external genitalia match the child's gender.

Some individuals use words such as "genderqueer" or "gender nonconforming," or several other terms (which will, of course, change over the years), to describe a non-binary gender. These individuals may express themselves in both masculine and feminine ways, or choose to float between genders (masculine one day and feminine the next). They may express no gender, or both genders at the same time. Some individuals may be interested in disrupting how society sees men and women. Other individuals who are genderqueer express a combination of genders because it's what feels right to them. Gender is a huge spectrum of possibilities.

Please also know that words are imprecise, and terms can change quickly. In whatever year you're reading this, there will be terms that are used that aren't used in 2017, when I'm writing this. Our 2017 terms may also be completely outdated. There may also be individuals who don't feel they fit within any of these terms or labels. We should never try to assign a label to anyone, because we wouldn't want a label assigned to us. If there's ever a question of what language to use to refer to someone, *ask them*. Ask about pronouns. Ask about their name. Then use what you're told to use. *Respect matters*.

This information will also change as cultural, social, and ideological (yes, ideological) definitions of the word *transgender* continue to grow. I hope these terms and ideas will help you make sense of how gender and sex interact in our culture. Gender affects us every single day, in a million different ways, and we owe it to our fellow human beings to accept them for the gender they are. In 2017, our culture is getting better at accepting and respecting folks, but we still have a long way to go. Hopefully you're part of that movement of acceptance and appreciation. If you took time to read this book, my guess is you are. Thanks for your kind and open heart.

***

I chose to write Gabe as a trans man because I read some short autobiographies from trans men, and I instantly respected and admired them. They were so fierce and centered in their identity, and I appreciated that determination more than I could articulate. I wanted to be proud enough to embrace myself in the same way. In 2015, I figured out why I felt such strong identification with their fierceness. It turns out I have ADHD, and when I made that discovery, a light bulb went on in my head—maybe in the same way it did for those men, when they figured out they were trans. This piece of knowledge changed my life, and it may have been the same for them. Now I recognize and claim who I am, just like those trans men claimed themselves. Of course, *having ADHD isn't the same as being transgender*. But I would argue there are parallels. Here's one: having ADHD is a whole-life situation. It's not just a school thing, or a work thing. It's an entirely different way to understand and interact with the world. Research agrees with me. And a sad one: now I understand what it feels like to be rejected for something I can't change. The hopeful parallel those trans men taught me? Whatever they might be, whether people agree or not, the inborn differences humans carry are beautiful, magical, and entirely awesome.

Here's one last fact for you. In survey results from 28,000 transgender US citizens, conducted in 2015 and published in 2016, the National Center for Transgender Equality told us that 40% of their survey respondents had tried to commit suicide. ***40%.*** In the general US population, the number of people who attempt suicide is under 5%. That 40% statistic haunts me, because Gabe is one of those people, as are some of my friends. Maybe you can do something to help make that statistic go down. Be kind. Be helpful if you know how to be. If you don't know how to help, ask someone who does, then get to work. Remember all individuals are worthy of love and respect.

Thanks for checking out Gabe's story. I'm glad you're here.

—Kirstin Cronn-Mills

If you are a LGBTQIA+ teen and you need help, please find it here. Please always remember you are not alone.

National Center for Transgender Equality
http://www.transequality.org

National Runaway Safeline
1-800-RUNAWAY
https://www.1800runaway.org

RECLAIM (Midwest/Minnesota-specific)
612-235-6743
http://reclaim.care

Trans Lifeline
1-877-565-8860
http://www.translifeline.org

Trans Student Educational Resources
http://www.transstudent.org

Trans Youth Equality Foundation
http://www.transyouthequality.org

The Trevor Project
1-866-488-7386
http://www.thetrevorproject.org

If you are a parent, guardian, teacher, or support person of a LGBTQIA+ youth, these resources might help you.

Gender Spectrum
https://www.genderspectrum.org

PFLAG
  Parents and Friends of Lesbians and Gays (supporting
  all LGBTQ+ individuals)
  https://www.pflag.org

Transgender Health Services, Program in Human Sexual-
  ity, University of Minnesota
  http://www.sexualhealth.umn.edu/clinic-center-sex-
  ual-health/transgender-health-services

Transgender Law Center
  510-587-9696
  https://transgenderlawcenter.org

Transparenthood
  http://transparenthood.net

WPATH
  World Professional Association for Transgender
  Health
  http://www.wpath.org

**If you are interested in reading books by transgender indi-
viduals, please check these resources.**

Biyuti Publishing
  https://publishbiyuti.org

Topside Press
  http://topsidepress.com

Trans-Genre Press
  http://trans-genre.net

Acknowledgments

This book took a village to bring it to life, and I'm blessed to have a very talented, kind village. My agent Amy Tipton believed in Gabe from the start, and I'm in her debt for it. Deep and humble love goes to Dan and Shae, for centering me, and to my Sisters In Ink, for making my work so much better. Thanks go to Johnny Hirschfeld, long-ago host of Beautiful Music for Ugly Children, for sharing the name with me, and also thanks to Dave Engen, for showing me how DJs do their jobs on tiny little radio stations like KMSU, where Johnny and Dave work(ed). Much gratitude goes to Bobby Ocean and Randal Morrison for helping me understand John, because they were part of radio when radio was king. Thanks go to Janet Reid, Joanna Volpe, Suzie Townsend, Stacey Barney, and Nick Healy, who helped with earlier drafts. Thanks go to Jenn Melby of the Coffee Hag, for allowing me to fictionalize her welcoming establishment. Of course, huge huge huge thanks and appreciation go to the folks at Flux: Brian Farrey-Latz, Lisa Novak, Bob Gaul, Sandy Sullivan, Steven Pomije, Marissa Pederson, and Courtney Colton.

Devoted thanks and love also go to my bio family, for teaching me that music is a joy and a necessity: Keith, Karna, and Kjell Cronn, Doris Cronn Patterson Nielsen-Eltoft, and Linda and James McGaffin.

My most profound appreciation goes to all the individuals who told me their stories so I could better understand Gabe. Without your generosity and trust, for which

I am humbled, there wouldn't be a book. This incredible crowd includes Katie B., Rhys and Julie G., Jaded Kate, Dean Kotula, Sophie M., Natasha, Alex Jackson Nelson, Jack, Christina Rose, Tavis R., and Lance W., as well as everyone who attended the Thursday night gender exploration group, including Erin, Hazel, and others who never told me their names. A deep and abiding thanks also goes to Janet Bystrom, who trusted me enough to let me visit the group, and who also reminded me that birthing a book is like birthing an identity—it's slow and complicated, but we can't give up.

About the Author

Kirstin Cronn-Mills' first novel, *The Sky Always Hears Me and the Hills Don't Mind*, was a finalist for the 2010 Minnesota Book Award for Young People's Literature. She teaches literature, writing, and critical thinking classes at South Central College in North Mankato, Minnesota, where she lives with her husband and son. Music has saved her more than once. Find her on the web at kirstincronn-mills.com.